Praise for
Black Girl in Paris

"A novel that, in its eroticism, shifting sexuality and vivid imagery, bears more than a little resemblance to *Soul Kiss*. Yet *Black Girl in Paris* in some ways is more daring, eschewing the comfortable imagery of the strong black woman who nurtured the protagonist of the earlier novel for the more complex and unpredictable set of guides who propel Eden's development."

—*Los Angeles Times*

"Paris in all of its possibilities and perils provides a backdrop for this singular exploration of maturity, angst, sexuality and personal identity." —*The Washington Post*

"More than anything else, *Black Girl in Paris* is the story of a quest, each station providing a necessary trial on Eden's road to encounter her own personal wizard, the quintessential expat, James Baldwin." —*The New York Times*

"Bold . . . The author tackles well-worn themes with refreshing directness and infuses the novel with unabashed, sometimes unsettling sexuality." —*Publishers Weekly*

"Ah, the intoxicating rapture of a first solo trip abroad. The exhilarating new vistas, the colorful customs, and the lip-smacking smorgasbord of awaiting vices . . . poetic . . . superb."

—*The Advocate*

"Sexy . . . dreamlike." —*The Village Voice*

(continued on next page . . .)

Also by Shay Youngblood

Soul Kiss

PLAN D'ASSEMBLAGE
DE PARIS

Mètres
Scale of Yards

Légende

Métropolitain
Ligne Nord-Sud

Les lettres A.B.C.D.E.F.G
renvoient aux plans de détail

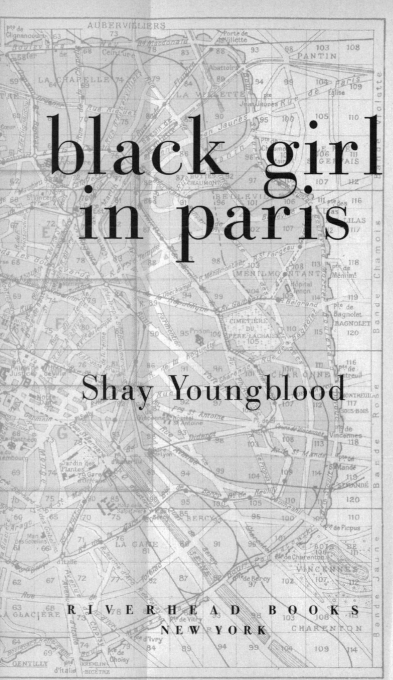

black girl in paris

Shay Youngblood

RIVERHEAD BOOKS
NEW YORK

RIVERHEAD BOOKS
Published by The Berkley Publishing Group
A division of Penguin Putnam Inc.
375 Hudson Street
New York, New York 10014

First Riverhead hardcover edition: January 2000
First Riverhead trade paperback edition: January 2001
Riverhead trade paperback ISBN: 1-57322-851-6

The Penguin Putnam Inc. World Wide Web site address is
http://www.penguinputnam.com

The Library of Congress has catalogued
the Riverhead hardcover edition as follows:

Youngblood, Shay.
Black girl in Paris : a novel / by Shay Youngblood.
p.   cm.
ISBN 1-57322-151-1
1. Afro-American women authors—France—Paris—Fiction.
2. Afro-American authors—France—Paris—Fiction.
3. Paris (France)—Intellectual life—Fiction.
4. Baldwin, James, date.   I. Title.
PS3575.08685 B58   2000   99-051679 CIP
813'.54—dc21

PRINTED IN THE UNITED STATES OF AMERICA

10 9 8 7 6 5 4 3 2 1

CONTENTS

To the angels, the poets, the lovers, and the thieves

If you go there in the place where it was, it will happen again; it will be there for you, waiting.

BELOVED, Toni Morrison

black girl
in paris

VEDETTES DU
PONT-NEUF
PARIS 1er
Tél. : 01 53 00 98 98

PLEIN TARIF
50 F

264333

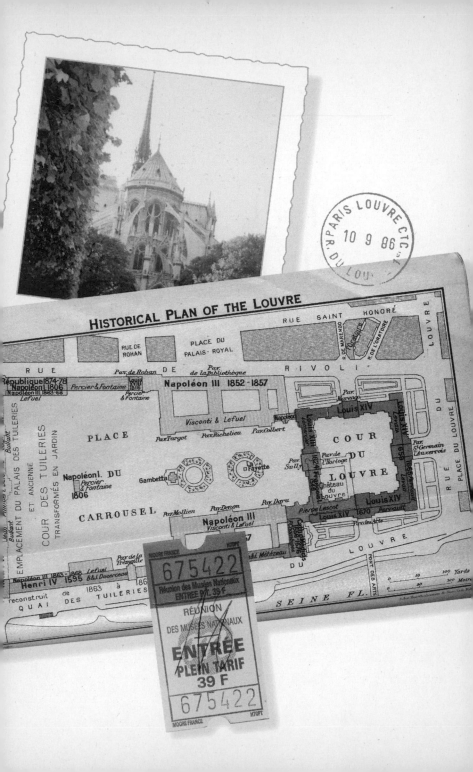

HISTORICAL PLAN OF THE LOUVRE

museum guide

Paris. September 1986. Early morning. She is lying on her back in a hard little bed with her eyes closed, dreaming in French. **Langston was here.** *There is a black girl in Paris lying in a bed on the fifth floor of a hotel in the Latin Quarter. Her eyes are closed against the soft pink dawn. Delicate maps of light line her face, tattoo the palms of her hands, the insides of her thighs, the soles of her feet like lace.* **Jimmy was here.** *She sleeps while small, feminine hands plant a bomb under the seat of a train headed toward the city of Lyon.*

James Baldwin, Langston Hughes, Richard Wright, Gabriel García Márquez and Milan Kundera all had lived in Paris as if it had been part of their training for greatness. When artists and writers spoke of Paris in their memoirs and letters home it

I

was with reverence. Those who have been and those who still dream mention the quality of the light, the taste of the wine, the *joie de vivre,* the pleasures of the senses, a kind of freedom to be anonymous and also new. I wanted that kind of life even though I was a woman and did not yet think of myself as a writer. *I was a mapmaker.*

I remember the long, narrow room, the low slanted ceiling, the bare whitewashed walls, the spotted, musty brown carpet. To my left a cracked porcelain sink with a spigot that ran only cold water. On its ledge a new bar of soap, a blue ragged-edged washcloth shaped like a pocket, and a green hand towel. A round window at the foot of the bed looked out onto the quai St-Michel, a street that runs along the Seine, a river flowing like strong coffee through the body of Paris. The *quai* was lined with book stalls and painters with their easels and wooden plates of wet fall colors.

I am there again. It's as if I have somebody else's eyes. The Paris at the foot of my bed looks as if it were painted leaf by leaf and stone by stone with tiny brushstrokes. People dressed in dark coats hurrying along the narrow sidewalks look like small black birds. Time is still when I look out at the pale, gray sky, down to the silvery river below, which by midmorning will be crowded with double-decker boats filled with tourists. In the river, on an island, I can see the somber face of Notre-Dame cathedral and farther down, an enormous, block-long, turreted, pale stone building that looks like a castle, but which I am told is part of the Palais de Justice, which houses in its basement the Conciergerie, the prison where Queen Marie Antoinette waited to have her head chopped off and the writer James Baldwin spent one night after being accused of stealing a hotel bedsheet. Even the prisons here are beautiful, and everything is so old. Back home you can see the bars on the windows of buildings and houses, so you know that they are prisons. Sometimes bondage is invisible.

The first time I woke up in Paris I thought I'd been wounded. My body ached that first morning. My eyes, nose, and lips were puffy, as if my face had been soaked in water. My skin was dry and ashy. My joints were tight. When I stretched the full length of my body, bones popped and crunched like loose pebbles in a jar. The dream I woke up with was like a first memory, the most vivid of all the old movies that projected themselves onto the me that was. I woke up with a piece of broken glass clutched in my left hand. There was a small spot of blood on the sheets underneath me.

Before I left home I cut my hair close to my scalp so I could be a free woman with free thoughts, open to all possibilities. I was making a map of the world. In ancient times maps were made to help people find food, water, and the way back home. I needed a map to help me find love and language, and since one didn't exist, I'd have to invent one, following the trails and signs left by other travelers. I didn't know what I wanted to be, but I knew I wanted to be the kind of woman who was bold, took chances, and had adventures. I wanted to travel around the world. It was my little-girl dream.

I woke up suddenly one morning, at dawn. As the light began to bleed between the blinds into my room, the blank wall in front of me dissolved into a colorful collage by Romare Bearden of a naked black woman eating a watermelon. Against the iridescent blue background lay the outline of the city of Paris. The woman was me. This was my first sign of the unusual shape of things to come. By the time I came back to myself I was booked on an Air France flight to Paris. Paris would kill me or make me strong.

In 1924 at the age of twenty-two, Langston Hughes, *the Negro Poet Laureate of Harlem,* author of *The Big Sea,* arrived in Paris with seven dollars in his pocket. He worked as a door-man, second cook, and dishwasher at a jazz club on rue Pigalle. He wrote blues poems and stories and lived a poet's life. He wrote about the joys of living as well as the heartache.

My name is Eden, and I'm not afraid of anything anymore. Like my literary godfathers who came to Paris before me, I intend to live a life in which being black won't hold me back.

Baldwin's prophetic essays . . . *The Fire Next Time* . . . *No Name in the Street* . . . *Nobody Knows My Name* . . . were like the sound of trumpets in my ears. Baldwin knew things that I hoped someday he would tell me. The issues in my mind were still black versus white, right versus wrong, good versus evil, and me against the world.

The spring before I arrived in Paris, the city was on alert. I cut out an article from a news magazine that listed the horrible facts: April 2, a bomb aboard a TWA plane exploded over Athens, killing four Americans; April 5, an explosion in a West Berlin disco killed an American soldier and a Turkish woman, 230 people were wounded; April 15, in retaliation, President Ronald Reagan bombed Muammar Qadaffi's headquarters in

Tripoli, killing fifteen civilians. Three American hostages were killed in Lebanon in response. April 17, a British woman was arrested in London's Heathrow airport, carrying explosives planted in her luggage by her Jordanian fiancé, who had intended to blow up a Tel Aviv–bound El Al flight. Terrorism was so popular that there were full-page ads in the *International Herald Tribune* offering hijacking insurance to frequent flyers.

I was no stranger to terrorism . . .

I was born in Birmingham, Alabama, where my parents witnessed the terror of eighteen bombs in six years. During that time the city was nicknamed Bombingham. When the four little girls were killed by a segregationist's bomb at church one Sunday morning in 1963, I had just started to write my name. I still remember writing theirs . . . *Cynthia* . . . *Addie Mae* . . . *Carole* . . . *Denise* . . . Our church sent letters of condolence to their families. We moved to Georgia, but I did not stop being afraid of being blown to pieces on an ordinary day if God wasn't looking. I slept at the foot of my parents' bed until I was eleven years old, when my mother convinced me that the four little girls were by now colored angels and would watch over me as I slept. But I didn't sleep much, and for most of my childhood I woke up each morning tired from so much running in my dreams—from faceless men in starched white sheets, from policemen with dogs, from firemen with water hoses. I was living in two places, night and day. In the night place I ran but they never caught me, and in the morning brown angels kissed my face. I woke up with tears on my pillow.

I was no stranger to terror . . .

When I was thirteen years old and living in Georgia I was in love with a girl in my class named Rosaleen and with her older brother, Anthony. Rosaleen and I played touching games in her bedroom, games she'd learned from her brother. We never spoke when we were naked and lying still on the carpet waiting for a hand to move an arm, bend a knee, for lips to kiss, for fingers to caress like feathers. We created still-life compositions with each other's pliant limbs, we were corpses, and for a few moments, a few hours, death seemed like something beautiful I wanted for the rest of my life. The fear of being caught heightened the sensations she awakened in me. Once when Anthony was home from college he sent Rosaleen downstairs to watch television, and he and I played the touching games. In Anthony's eyes I was a pretty brown-skinned girl. He whispered a continuous stream of compliments about my strange narrow eyes, my soft, still tender new breasts that filled his hands. He called me "Sugar Mama." His hands were rough, his smell musky and rank. I didn't struggle against the thick fingers that pushed between my legs, but let the hardness search the stillness inside of me. My feelings about Rosaleen and Anthony created a confusion in me, a terror of choosing. Anthony touched my body, but Rosaleen was the one I wanted to touch me inside. I was afraid to lose Rosaleen, but eventually I did. She got pregnant by a boy she met at the county fair. The baby was sickly and soon died. Rosaleen was sent away to live with relatives in Philadelphia. I never saw her again, but I had been touched by her in a way that would make all other touches fade quickly. After Rosaleen and Anthony I was terrified that no one would ever love me again, that desire was a bubble that would burst when I touched it. Years later I met Leo, who loved my body for a while, then left me when I felt I needed him most.

A bomb can kill you instantly, love can make you wish you were dead.

Within days of my arrival in Paris four separate explosions killed three people and wounded 170. There was an atmosphere of paranoia. The tension was visible in people's eyes. Everyone was suspicious. Every abandoned bag standing alone for more than a few minutes could be filled with explosives set to kill. Anyone could be a terrorist. Bombs were exploding all over the city the fall I arrived, and that made tickets to Paris cheap and suicide unnecessary. I would become a witness. I left my body and another me took over, someone who had no fear of bombs or dying.

It is 1986. I am twenty-six years old. I have 140 dollars folded flat and pressed into my shoes between sock and sole. It is what's left of the 200 dollars I arrived with two days ago. I have no friends here and barely remember my two years of college French. I think that my ticket to Paris will be the beginning or the end of me.

In 1948 James Baldwin, author of *Another Country,* then twenty-five years old, arrived in Paris with forty dollars. During the Sixties civil rights movement he led marches, protests, and voter registration drives. His angry, articulate essays on race shocked France and compelled witnesses to action. He was awarded the medal of Legion of Honor by the French government. *I was a witness.*

Josephine Baker arrived in 1925, at age eighteen. She danced naked except for a string of bananas around her waist, sang the "Marseillaise" in beaded gowns, and was decorated by the French government for her efforts during World War II. She created a new tribe in her château with children from every ethnic group. Like the character she played in the film *Princess Tam Tam,* she represented to the French the exotic black, sexually independent woman who could learn to speak French and pick up enough manners to dine with royalty.

I was transformed.

Bricktop arrived penniless and taught Paris how to dance the Charleston. Richard Wright was already a celebrity; he joined the French intellectuals and gave voice to the Negro problem in America. There were others and there will be more. My heroes. They dared to make a way where there was none, and I want to be just like them.

I was born again.

This is the place where it happened, where it will happen again.

For once I slept without dreaming. I woke up when the plane touched down on the runway and heard the entire cabin clap and cheer the pilot and crew for our safe landing. As we taxied along the runway I pulled my small French-English dictionary out of my bag to look up in the phrase section how to take a cab. Across the aisle from me was a young woman who had slept through most of the flight. She was blonde with olive skin and had a long face and pretty features. She wore jeans and a black sweater and held a Museum of Modern Art gift bag in one hand and a large Louis Vuitton satchel on her lap. The satchel looked real, not like the imitations everyone at home wanted. I assumed she was American.

"It's my first time in Paris. What's the best way to get to the city? Is there a bus?"

"We can share a taxi if you like. Where are you going?" Her French accent was a surprise.

"I don't know. I was going to ask the driver for a hotel. I don't have much money."

She looked at me as if I was crazy.

"You don't know anyone?"

I shook my head.

"It will be very difficult to find something not expensive." She pursed her lips and blew into the air, a French gesture I would come to recognize and imitate. She said that the students would be arriving for classes that week.

"Many of the hotels not too dear will be . . . *complet*. You understand?"

I quickly flipped through my dictionary and learned that the hotels would be full, no vacancies.

"My name is . . . *Je m'appelle Eden.*"

"Delphine. Come," she commanded. We got up and joined the line of passengers exiting the plane. Charles de Gaulle airport was a maze of lines, people talking fast, signs I couldn't understand, and everywhere, guards carrying machine guns and holding fierce-looking dogs on short leashes. Then I began to be a little afraid of what I had done. I didn't know anyone, my

French was practically nonexistent, and I had only enough money to last a few weeks until I found a job. But there was no going back. I took a deep breath and followed Delphine to baggage claim. I was relieved to see my duffel bag circle round in front of me. We stood in long, crooked lines in customs. One for citizens of France and several for everyone else. I gave Delphine twenty dollars to change into francs for me. She said she would meet me outside. When she was out of sight I had the fleeting thought that at home I would never be stupid enough to give a stranger money and watch her walk away, but I was in Paris and I was giving myself up to new angels.

When I offered up my passport, the customs officer, who had had a dry, grim expression for all the passengers before me, looked at me, then back at my passport. He scanned my short natural hair, high forehead, slow, sleepy eyes, broad nose, and full lips, as if to make sure the brown-skinned girl in his hands was me. He pushed my passport toward me and startled me by speaking in English. "Welcome to France, mademoiselle. Enjoy your visit."

During the ride to the city Delphine told me that she was a student at the "Science Po," the Ecole des Sciences Politiques, which I later learned was comparable to Harvard. She wanted to be a lawyer and in the current term she was studying English. When I told her I was a writer her eyes grew large and she could not hide her admiration, as if seeing in me something special she had not noticed before.

"I admire the dedication of the artist, but nothing is certain for you. I am not so brave." She looked out the window.

I did not feel brave, there was nothing else I thought I could do or that held my interest in the same way. The taxi was an old white Mercedes with a gray leather interior. The driver looked African and spoke French. We had loaded our bags in the trunk and got inside. Delphine had given the driver an address and instructions in rapid French. We sat in silence looking out at early morning Paris. The cars on the highway seemed to go faster than in the States. I was so tired I kept nodding off. When the taxi stopped on busy rue de l'Université, in front of a photography shop, I opened my wallet and Delphine took out some of the bills she had exchanged for me and added some of her own.

She pointed out the Sorbonne from the foot of the hill before we turned into the lobby of her apartment building. I followed her up four flights of stairs. She opened the door onto a small studio with high ceilings and cream-colored walls that made the room seem much bigger than it really was. Books and a small compact-disc collection lined the longest wall in the small but neat room, a high-tech stereo system and a small TV found space there as well. A bare desk sat in front of the windows, overlooking the street. Two double futons were stacked on top of each other in a corner. The most beautiful feature of the room was the set of tall French windows covered by metal shutters. Delphine opened the windows, letting in the light and noise of the street below. I went to the windows and looked down into the street. I saw a shop displaying cartons of brightly colored fruit, a florist's shop with spring in huge vivid bouquets that brightened the gray morning. She pointed me in the direction of the toilet. The bathroom fixtures were odd and ancient-looking. I did not recognize my face in the smoky gilt-framed mirror above the wide porcelain sink. There were dark circles under my eyes and my hair was so short. It was still me, a new me in a new place ready to begin again. I felt lost. After my father's funeral I felt as if I were drifting inside, as if anyone could disappear. Few things were certain. *My father was dead.*

Delphine made us strong cups of coffee in the tiny red-and-white kitchen area—miniature appliances lined up under tall cabinets. Stale bread crumbs were scattered over the counter, a knife left sticking out of a pot of butter. We added sugar to the coffee and drank it black from heavy yellow bowls.

"What will you do?" she asked, sitting crosslegged on the futons next to me.

"I thought I could look for a job as a secretary or an au pair." I sipped the coffee and felt the caffeine spreading through my chest.

"I have heard the American Church has a place to look for jobs. I can check the newspaper for you. There is a black American writer who is every day at a bookstore close to here. He might help you. I think he is a poet."

Delphine made two phone calls, then we left the apartment to look for a room. Her apartment was in the heart of the Latin Quarter, near the boulevard St-Michel. The streets were filled with people even though it was still early in the morning. Delphine was right, the less expensive hotels in the guidebook were *complet,* and I could not afford the more expensive ones. I could see that she felt pity for me and that she was determined to help me. Perhaps she thought an artist who was destined for a life of poverty needed all the help she could get. It started to rain, and as we were walking along the Seine back to her apartment I saw a hotel with a tiny sign in the window. By some miracle they had one room left, for about thirty-five dollars a night. We were told that it did not have a toilet, I'd have to share one on the floor below, and if I wanted to take a shower it would cost me about three dollars. The shower was in a stone cubicle in the basement. The clerk was a young man who, when he realized I was American, began speaking to me in English. This was a small relief to me, knowing I'd soon be on my own. I agreed without even seeing the room. I only hoped it had a view. It was not far from Delphine's apartment. She helped me carry my bags back to the hotel.

Delphine gave me her phone number and told me to call her when I was settled. She was going away to visit her sister in Lyon for a week until school started. Her cousin Jean-Michel would be in her apartment until she returned and he spoke a little English, so if I needed help I was to call him. I reached out to hug her but she leaned only her face toward me. She kissed me on each cheek and wished me *bonne chance*. She was the one who would need the luck. The very next day a bomb was found on a train headed toward Lyon. It was defused and no one was hurt, but it was only the first sign of more danger to come.

Suddenly it was night, and I was far from home and completely alone. The little room at the top of the stairs was not decorated with a chandelier, gold-leafed antiques, and a canopy bed covered in delicate lace as I'd imagined, but I was thankful to have a place indoors to sleep. On the floor at the foot of the bed were my green duffel bag and a black canvas backpack, which contained everything I owned. A tiny book of Bible verses the size of a matchbook, a *1968 Frommer's Guide to Paris* I'd stolen from the public library. I knew all the major attractions by heart. I used the guide as a dream journal, writing between the lines. Between the pages I filed found poems and movie stubs and photographs. There was the gold pen from Dr. Bernard, three sharp number two pencils, a red Swiss army knife, seven pairs of white cotton panties, two pairs of white socks and one pair of black tights, a navy blue sweater and a pair of black jeans, a fat, palm-sized French-English dictionary, and a new address book with three addresses written in it. On the chair next to the sink, a pair of black stretch pants, a pair of gold hoop earrings, a watch with a thick brown leather band, a green trench coat from a military surplus store, and underneath the chair, a pair of black leather sneakers.

"Je m'appelle Eden. Je suis une . . . writer." The new me tried to impress the scratched mirror. I couldn't remember the French word for writer. *Ecrivain.* I said other things in French and practiced forgetting my old life.

My mother told me that she found me lying there, like a lost book or a forgotten hat. Found me crying, hungry, wet, and cold, wrapped in newspaper at the bottom of a brown paper bag in the bathroom of a Greyhound bus station. My father confirmed her story.

"Who am I?"

"Mama's little girl."

"Who am I?"

"Daddy's African princess."

"How do you know for sure?"

I discover that nothing is ever certain. A name, a birthday, an entire life can be invented, and that being so, can be changed. I intended to change all the ordinary things about myself. When I began to write I kept secret diaries, writing between the lines of books my father found in the trash at work. Books on law and economics, typewriter manuals. I wrote about the life I lived in the night place, where I traveled as far as the stars. Before I could speak my father read to me from his found books, sounding out each word as if it were an island, as if either of us understood. Having learned to read so late in life he valued books as treasures of knowledge waiting to be unlocked.

When I was four years old my parents told me that I was an orphan. My parents were orphans too. They found each other in church one Sunday. Hermine was a big-boned, sturdy, pecan-colored woman, with green eyes and gray hair she kept braided and wrapped around her head. She taught Prior Walker how to read the Bible, and in return he worshiped her. He was small for a man, with thick, callused hands, and balding by the time he was twenty-three. She was a seamstress in a blue-jean factory, and he was the custodian at a bank. They were old, like grandparents. Kind and patient, hardworking Christians. They were alone in the world until they found me. Their family, and therefore mine, was the church. We were happy together. They called me Eden. I made dresses for my dolls, but I was more interested in reading books and writing poems than in sewing. One summer Hermine and I pieced together a quilt made from scraps of clothes Prior and Hermine had worn out or I had outgrown. She called it the family circle quilt. The center image was three interlocking circles. She cried when it was done and sewed a lock of hair from each of us into three corners of the quilt, and in the fourth corner she sewed a secret. She folded the quilt into quarters and packed it into the cedar chest at the foot of her bed. In winter when it was time for me to go to sleep, she pulled the covers up around my chin.

"When you have a family you can put your baby to sleep under your family circle."

"My baby will have pretty dreams," I said stroking the lines of thread so lovingly handstitched.

"As long as Singer makes sewing machines, we'll get by," Hermine always said. The old machine she had must have been one of the first Singers, made in the late 1800s. She had a new electric model my father had bought her for her birthday, but for the quilt we used the one her mother left her before she died. Hermine told the same story about how her life began over and over again. At the age of two she had been left on the doorstep of a colored orphanage along with a note and the old Singer sewing machine in its case next to where she lay asleep. This was all she knew, but her life was full of stories she made up as she went along.

The only other family we had was Aunt Victorine, my mother's best friend and mine. On the first Saturday morning of each month she used to take me for blessings to the Church of Modern Miracles, where we both pretended she was my mother. When we were together she called me Daughter and I called her Mother, and that was only one of our secrets. Aunt

Vic had never married and was childless, and in her way adopted me so that I had two mothers. She had something to do with my wanting to go to Paris. From the time she showed me on a map she drew with a broken pencil on her kitchen wall and told me that black people were free in Paris. Free to live where you wanted, work where you were qualified, and love whom you pleased. At least that was the rumor she had heard. One of her friends in Chicago, where she had grown up, had a sister, an opera singer who went to Paris and married a white man. The opera singer became famous in Europe. According to Aunt Vic the white folks in America didn't want us to know about that kind of living, where a colored person could socialize and marry whom they wanted whether they were white or black, Chinese or Hindu. If she could have chosen, Aunt Vic surely would not have chosen to be a maid for most of her life. She worked two days a week for a rich white doctor in Green Island Hills. That was freedom to her, to choose the life you wanted to live.

"And who would not choose to live well?" Aunt Vic said.

Aunt Vic's stories about Paris had sounded like fantasies. She talked about it as if it were a made-up place. If Paris was a real place, I wanted to go.

"Every day you ought to learn something new, Daughter," Aunt Vic said. I tried to learn new things, and I wrote them down like recipes between the lines of my found books.

I would go to stay with Aunt Vic, who returned me home Sunday morning ready for Sunday school with Hermine and Prior. I slept through most of Sunday morning sermons at the First African Baptist Missionary Church, where the service was orderly, the hymns hushed, and the service short, and nobody cried too loud or shouted that the Holy Ghost had them by the collar. There was no dancing in the aisles. At the Church of Modern Miracles there was a three-piece band—drums, electric organ, and electric guitar—and several ladies in the front row who shook tambourines and their ample hips and tremulous breasts all through the service. People shouted, praised God so their prayers could be heard above the sins of the city, were possessed by the Holy Spirit, who took over their bodies, shaking them with emotion and filling their eyes with tears and their throats with hallelujahs. I could use my voice strong and was put in the young people's choir. Soon I was singing a solo almost every Saturday morning. And Aunt Victorine had me performing at the age of six in juke joints on dirt roads for miles around almost every Saturday night. After midnight, when a juke joint was most crowded, some cigar-smelling man would lift me up onto a table in the middle of the room and somebody else would unplug the jukebox. Sometimes there would be a pianist or a guitar player to accompany me. I would sing songs I'd heard on Aunt Vic's record player. Aunt Vic taught me how to lift the hem of my dress and dance at the end of the song like Josephine Baker and the French can-can dancers who looked so glamorous in the photographs she showed me. The audience would throw handfuls of change and crumpled dollar bills at my dancing feet. I loved the attention. I dreamed about doing the can-can in Paris. If Mama hadn't found out when I was thirteen, I might've become a star on the dirt-floor circuit. Instead I started taking classical voice lessons from a mean old Creole woman who used to be an entertainer. Her long black curls left greasy spots on the collars of her old-fashioned quilted pastel dressing gowns. Miss Candy shouted at me in Creole when I forgot the words to a song. I didn't like her and the lessons didn't last long. Aunt Vic didn't speak to Mama for a long time. She was mad at losing all that income from my singing. And she missed me as much as I missed her. Low lights, Aunt Vic's copper-colored lipstick, and the sparkling dresses she let me borrow to perform in made me dream of a kind of life different from the one I was living. I made maps in my mind that would lead to other worlds.

Aunt Vic loved to be read to. She had grown up in Chicago and still had a subscription to the *Chicago Defender* so she could keep up with the community even though she had left under duress. The circumstances of her leaving the North many years before remained a mystery to me even though I asked her every time she started talking about the old days. Once I got her to admit her leaving had something to do with a man she didn't care to dance with, a gangster who owned the club she worked in. Aunt Vic loved Langston Hughes's Simple stories, which were published in the *Chicago Defender* from 1943 to 1966, Aunt Vic said. His main character, Jesse B. Simple, was everyman, every black man, and she loved him.

"Jesse B. Simple is real, I think that's a real person. I knew somebody just like that back in Chicago. Munro Fish, a sweet-talking jailbird who truly believed that someday he would run for a government office. He had it all figured out just like Simple. Always talking about race."

She had collected all the stories. She cut them out of the newspaper, and every once in a while she would pull them out and I'd read to her. The language was a little salty, but Mama wasn't around to get holy. Simple would talk about having Indian blood, and Aunt Vic would add her commentary.

"Like what Southern Negro don't claim that?" She would laugh. We would start packing our bags when he talked about all the colored people in Harlem. She would start singing about speakeasies and going up to Harlem like we were hearing the story for the first time.

The stories made us laugh and feel like we knew what was going on in the world, and we had a lot of our own opinions about that.

Aunt Vic showed me pictures of her old life as a dancer, the girls who went to France, and Josephine Baker, who was to her a symbol of complete freedom. I made up stories and acted out little dramas for my parents, playing all the parts myself. I wrote sad poems about orphans, and I moved through my life taking pictures with a toy camera, recording things in my mind, writing them down between the lines of other books. One day I made up my mind that I would go to Paris to be free.

When I was thirteen my parents gave me a typewriter, for which they had made many sacrifices. I typed my first novel in fourteen days. I wrote all the stories I knew and made up new ones. I typed them and put them in my library, a small bookshelf next to my bed that my father had made and my mother had painted yellow. By then I was reading in the adult section of the library and was certain after reading Langston Hughes's autobiography, *The Big Sea,* that I wanted to be a writer and feast at the banquet of life. Going to Paris would be an hors d'oeuvre. I kept my thoughts pressed between the lines of biology texts and biographies of dead presidents that no one else ever checked out anyway.

The color rust tastes like dirt, and my bones ache. The first blood on my fingers tastes like new nickels. Help me. I stumble on new legs into rooms so full of static sparks fly from my fingertips. As I reach for a vowel with my lips, an "O" softly escapes into the dry air. I need someone to introduce me to the woman who woke up in my skin. Mother, may I? Maman, puis-je?

"My body is breaking," says the me who is not my mother's child.

"It will bend," the mother whispers.

When I got my first blood, my mother told me I was a woman. There was something false about her happiness. Her joy came with conditions that must be followed.

"Don't let boys touch you." Anthony was a man.

"Be a sweet girl." I was hard candy.

My father pushed me off his lap and my mother seemed blind to me. Aunt Vic was my salvation.

"Being a woman is a cross we women must bear," she said.

"When I go to Paris I will leave behind the little orphan girl and all I will take with me is her body and some of her clothes. I'll make maps so other people can get there too, adventurers like me."

This was my little-girl dream.

Before Paris, at university, I studied English literature, and all it was good for in the end was a job as a librarian.

I wanted to hold on to old things, but I wanted new things to make me forget. When I was twenty-five I found a job in the house of dead things. Villa Luisa, known locally as the Dimple Mansion, built by the richest black man born into slavery. The house recalled an Italian villa and had become a museum and a memorial to a family of successful African American entrepreneurs. I was hired by the museum's director to assist him in giving tours and cataloging the collection. The director, Dr. Edgar Bernard, was a serious, scholarly gentleman and looked the part. He was tall, gray-haired, and elegant. His old-fashioned wire-rimmed glasses accented wide eyes that popped from his head like lightbulbs. He wore the same dark gray suit and a crisp white shirt every day. His silk ties looked like pieces of stained-glass windows. The director was a lonely man. He spoke quietly and quickly as if afraid I would lose interest or he would forget to tell me something important as he veered into heated dissertations on obscure areas of Greek and African civilization. I was fascinated and listened to him with my whole body as if to memorize his knowledge.

When Dr. Bernard spoke there were secrets in his voice. I knew because I had secrets of my own. Dead things locked in a box I kept out of sight. I listened to his lonely, his hurt, and his misunderstood. He had dedicated his life to preserving a dignified memory of his mentor.

Dr. Bernard was a young man when he met Mason Dimple and became his secretary. Dimple sent him to Yale. They traveled the world together.

"Mr. Dimple gave me my first job. I worked in his garden every summer from the time I was fourteen years old. He sent me to school. I studied anthropology, receiving my doctorate just a few months before Mr. Dimple died.

" 'Edgar,' he said, 'You have worked very hard and I've had to work hardly at all. I hope that you will make of your life something beautiful.' Mason was very good to me." Dr. Bernard's eyes got misty and his voice softened even more when he talked about Mr. Dimple, whom he sometimes, slipping, called Mason.

Now Dr. Bernard was married to a large woman who wore too much makeup and laughed too loudly. They were childless. The few times I saw her at holiday parties Mrs. Bernard's sadness and disappointment were clear as the champagne glasses she kept filled to the top.

Everything in the Villa was dead or old except me. The offices were in the basement of Mason Dimple's yellow brick mansion. The house was surrounded by a meticulously manicured landscape of pink and white dogwoods, red and orange azalea bushes, and wine-colored Japanese maples. Inside, the furnishings were opulent, each of the twenty-six rooms decorated in a different period. On the ceiling of each room were painted re-creations of religious scenes by Michelangelo from the Sistine Chapel. Angels floated above our heads all day. The Dimples were not religious, but they had wanted to impress their guests with their culture acquired from trips abroad. The house had marble bathrooms with gold fixtures and bronze-and-crystal chandeliers. The floors were inlaid with rare wood or covered in rare Oriental carpets. English antiques in the living room, French baroque velvet sofas in the sitting room.

A white marble statue of a naked muscled Greek god stood

in the foyer, a replica of a famous sculpture in the Louvre. The director had placed a discreet bronze ivy leaf over its private parts after several church groups complained that the statue disturbed the children on tours.

Mason Dimple's bedroom was not included on the tour. Dr. Bernard said that Mason Dimple was so consumed with grief when his parents died in a train wreck when he was almost twenty-one that he stayed in his room for seven days staring into the flame of a candle, trying to pray them back to life. Then he painted his bedroom walls black. When I opened the door to his bedroom I could feel his suffering like cold fingers on the back of my neck. It was like standing in an opulent prison cell.

The Villa held a large collection of European art, English silver, and Greek sculpture. Most museum patrons expected to see a collection of African art because of Mason Dimple's race. But there was nothing African here except a wooden mask from Nigeria half eaten by termites and a few Moroccan tapestries. Mason Dimple hated anything too black or too African. At one time he had wanted to be a part of local white society. He thought his money and barely brown skin would allow him access, but he soon realized that he was not welcome. He made do with occasional contact with the black bourgeoisie that mirrored white society with its balls and charity events.

Dr. Bernard took me on a tour of the house and gave me facts I memorized. The questions from our guests were always the same.

When was the house built? Who was the architect?
How did the family make its fortune?
How did they die?

Why did Mason Dimple never marry or have children?

What are the naked wrestlers on the Greek vase in the study doing?

These were the things Dr. Bernard instructed me to say to the busloads of curious foreign tourists and rowdy school children and locals who had always wondered what went on inside the yellow brick mansion on Dimple Court.

In 1933 Mason's father, Simon Dimple, was the richest black man in the state of Georgia. He had spent his youth as a house slave on a plantation owned by his white father. He had been taught to cook by his mother, who was the plantation cook. He ran away from home when he was thirteen years old and earned his way in the world as a cook for rich white Northern college students. He met his future wife, Daisy, an octoroon girl from Louisiana, on a train in New York. They both were passing for white. He fell in love with her, and they returned to Georgia. He used Daisy and her brothers, who also passed for white, to purchase land and hire labor to build a restaurant on the outskirts of a growing town. They quietly ran the business behind the scenes and joined the local elite black community. Neither Daisy nor Simon could eat in the dining room of their own restaurant because it was for whites only. It was very popular and enabled Simon to invest in other businesses and real estate and make a fortune. The Dimples' firstborn child, Mason, they sent away to boarding school in Switzerland from the time he was a small boy to shelter him from the pain of racism. He spent summers with his family and eventually went to Yale, graduating with a degree in business.

At Simon Dimples' Plantation Restaurant, black women,

dressed like Aunt Jemima in red-and-white checkered head kerchiefs, voluminous skirts, and white aprons, served the white patrons with a grin and a shuffle. The entire kitchen staff was made up of black men in white uniforms. The food was old-fashioned Southern cooking. Fried chicken, collard greens, sweet potatoes, macaroni and cheese, chicken and dumplings, lemon cheesecakes, blackberry cobblers, rice puddings, barbecued ribs, biscuits and cornbread. As good as the food was, that was not why the restaurant was so popular. It was the novelty of whites being served in the manner of their ancestors by a wait staff that reminded them of the good old days. The Dimples were members of the NAACP even though many members protested that the Dimples' restaurant perpetuated the stereotype of a slave plantation, where the white masters were still being served by happy blacks.

The Dimples considered themselves good and patriotic Americans. They raised the flag on holidays, bought war bonds, and wanted the world to see them as they saw themselves—successful, sophisticated citizens who contributed to their community. The Dimples were generous philanthropists, donating large sums of money to their church and black colleges and medical facilities all over the South. They were good businessmen and, after his parents died, Mason Dimple sold the offensive restaurant and most of the other properties. He set up a foundation to ensure the preservation of his home as a memorial to his parents after his own death.

A year after Mason Dimple himself died, the board of directors he had set up was ready to hire someone to organize the home's collection. My first job was to catalog everything in the house and develop a system for marking. First I looked through the photographs. Mason seemed to have been a happy child, in short velvet pants, white ruffled shirts, and high buttoned boots. As he grew older his smiles faded to a hard line and he wore pressed tailored suits and posed stiffly for the camera's eye. He still looked like a boy even after his hair had thinned and his small rimless glasses sat on his nose like little windows.

Under the stairs in the basement of the dead man's house there were several boxes of books Dr. Bernard didn't seem to know existed. One rainy afternoon when tours were slow and Dr. Bernard was attending a conference at a downtown hotel, I opened one of the boxes and flipped through the pages of historical novels and murder mysteries that Mason was so fond of. Behind the boxes was a small trunk half hidden by a large, brightly patterned rug. I dragged the trunk into my office and opened it. Inside were a packet of letters and several photographs. In the photographs Mason Dimple's eyes seemed happy only once. In one photograph he was walking through a flock of birds in a square in Venice. He was smiling at a young man who faintly resembled Dr. Bernard and who seemed to be flapping his arms to make the birds fly. There was a well-dressed young woman in the picture. She was wearing a tall hat and stood nearby watching both men with a weary, tight little smile.

The tiny black leather notebook fit in the palm of my hand. I found it sewn inside a linen bag in a secret compartment in Mason Dimple's traveling office trunk designed by Louis Vuitton in the mid 1800s. It was slender, the leather was smooth to touch, and inside, each page overflowed with tiny black lines like marching ants. The words were crowded together carefully as if they had been written in a small, dark place by someone with plenty of time, lots to say, and no one to listen. My hands were trembling as I cut open the neat stitches with my pocket knife. As archivist for the house museum where Mason Dimple was born and died I had access to every silver spoon and faded photograph that made up his life. Mason Dimple was a complicated man, there was no doubt about that. He had wanted to be a poet and so he went where poets went, tried to live as they did, but his money got in the way. He died a bachelor with no heirs and left a substantial fortune in a trust that would preserve the family home and the Dimple name forever.

I wanted to be a poet and I knew early on, but it was not practical for a girl born into a poor family to be a poet. At first I studied biology in preparation for life as a nurse. This was to ease my parents' minds that I would be able to take care of myself, but I became fascinated with history and poetry and the lives of artists. I was never a practical girl. Five years out of college I found myself working in the basement of a dead man's house, sorting through intimate details of his life, discovering common ground.

The letters were faded, but I could read the words, which told a story different from the one I recited to visitors to the house. It was in his handwriting. I knew it from the dull entries in the diaries I had cataloged. Places visited, foods eaten, and the prices in local currency of gifts purchased.

There were love letters:

*My tongue is wasted on words when you would be of
better use in my mouth.*

There were rooms full of secrets:
The Great Hall, where the family received guests and gave
lovely parties.

*Mother made me scrub the floors on my hands and
knees this morning as she recited prayers for my sinful
soul.*

The music room, where the family entertained their guests.

*Mother tied me to the piano bench until I could play
perfectly. Finally my fingers behaved. What a bad boy
to make Mother unhappy. She speaks French when
she is unhappy.*

The master bedroom, where the father slept.

*It is curious how Father never sleeps alone at night,
nor does he sleep with Mother.*

The pink bedroom, where the mother slept.

She cries at night. Her weeping is my lullaby.

Mason Dimple's bedroom, closed to visitors.

He is my first love and will be my last. I would be lost
without him.

Mason Dimple had many secrets. Secrets I did not tell visitors to the house. Sometimes when it was quiet in the house I could hear a young woman singing and a grown man weeping. I could feel the cold, sad suffering of a mother's love. Some nights I dreamed, some nights I didn't sleep at all. My dreams shift my thinking:

> *I am in Paris. I climb a spiral staircase seven flights*
> *up. I enter a room made entirely of books, the walls,*
> *the fireplace, and the ceiling. The floor is a soft carpet*
> *of words. Leatherbound books with* SECRETS *etched in*
> *gold leaf along their spines are displayed in elaborate*
> *boxes set in the walls behind glass. The smell is haunt-*
> *ing, dried ink and musty memories. I lie on the floor*
> *and words beneath me whisper in my ear, water*
> *words, the names of trees and flowers, parts of the*
> *body, parts of the eye. I leave the room and enter a*
> *dark hallway heading toward the light. I see my father*
> *in the distance, he waves me back toward the living.*
> *I whisper good-bye and turn my back on him.*

My father died of a heart attack the summer before I went to Paris. All of us who knew him almost died from shock. A pious deacon of the church. A kind neighbor. A loving husband and father. Simply put: a good man gone to glory. "Prior Walker, dearly beloved" was carved in stone. Daddy was stitched onto the tender parts of my heart. My body folded and water fell from my eyes like rain.

The weight of all those dead things pulled me down.

One afternoon shortly after my father died, I had a revelation and a sign. The streets outside were steaming as if little teapots were brewing beneath the city, but I was cool underground. I was working at my desk in the windowless basement office. That morning the principal from a local boy's school called to cancel their one o'clock tour, and I was afraid I would cry all afternoon. A man I'd been dating had called me at noon to tell me he was returning to Detroit. He'd been looking for a job as a radio news journalist the whole year I knew him, but he had been unlucky and he felt that it was time for us both to face facts. For me the reality was more jarring, that he hadn't even asked me to go with him, let alone marry him. I couldn't say I was in love with him. I was just sad to be by myself again. I wanted to run away from so much loss all at once.

I was not allowed to be with my sadness for long. At one-fifteen the front doorbell rang. I went up the stairs, crossed the foyer, and opened the front door. Standing there were a regal-looking, well-dressed older black woman wearing heavy gold jewelry and too much powder on her face and a younger man in a conservative dark suit who I guessed by their resemblance was her son. I invited them in and noticed that they spoke with soft West Indian accents. The son seemed more interested in the house than the mother. Sometimes he would whisper to her in what sounded like French. I gave them the standard tour and the son asked the standard questions. At the end of the tour the son looked around with a puzzled expression.

"I presume that Mr. Dimple was an educated man."

"Yes, he graduated from Yale."

"That is not what I mean. His collection seems incomplete. He traveled to Africa in the Fifties?"

"Yes, but he wasn't much interested in African art. He brought back several tapestries from Morocco, and you saw the Ibo mask?"

The man made a noise in his throat and pitched his eyes around the room once more. "You can tell so much about a man by what he keeps in his house."

"Thank you very much for the tour. It was lovely," the mother said, signing the guest book. I noticed she wrote down Paris as her address.

"How did you hear about the museum?" I asked, curious.

"The concierge at the hotel recommended it."

"Are you West Indian?"

"We are *French*," the mother said, as if I'd insulted her.

The son looked at me as if seeing me for the first time. His eyes assessed me quickly, lingering on my breasts before returning to my face. He seemed to want to continue talking with me.

"There are many black Americans living in Paris, many artists," the son said. "I believe the black American writer James Baldwin makes his home in France. Do you know him?" he asked, as if it were possible for me to know someone famous.

"I know his work. I've been listening to my aunt go on about France since I was a little girl. I'd love to go there someday."

The son warmed to me when I said I wanted to be a writer. He said there were many bohemian artists living in Paris.

"There are certainly enough entertainers," the mother said, dabbing at her perspiring nose with a delicate lace handkerchief.

For the next half hour the son, Maxime Bazille, and his mother, Madame Marie-Lise Bazille, convinced me that Paris was the last red apple on the highest branches of a tree well worth climbing. I thanked them, and for the first time Paris became a real destination, with real places to eat, museums to see, and wide boulevards to stroll. A list of inexpensive hotels, bakeries and cafés, clothing shops and museums neatly printed in Maxime Bazille's elegant hand was folded in my pocket.

By six o'clock that evening the security guard hadn't shown up. I called Dr. Bernard and offered to lock up the house and set the alarm. He agreed, and I began clearing up my desk. I called a local copy shop to find out how much they charged for passport photos. Before setting the alarm I went into the library, and my eyes fell on several books by James Baldwin. I'd seen them every day, but that evening it was as if a laser beam pointed them out to me and I was drawn to them. Each of the books was a signed first edition. *Giovanni's Room, Another Country, Go Tell It on the Mountain, Nobody Knows My Name, The Fire Next Time*. Each book was signed, "Affectionately, Jimmy." I sat in Mason Dimple's reading chair and read into the night, from one book to the next. The most brilliantly illuminating passages were underlined with blue ink. By the time the sun came up, my eyes were red and tired and an overwhelming sadness had clouded the room. When Dr. Bernard arrived he thought I was sleeping. He touched my shoulder and called my name.

His eyes fell on the bundle of love letters on the table next to me.

"I found them behind the stairs."

Dr. Bernard sat facing me in a leather wing chair, wearily, as if it were the end of a long day and not the beginning.

"After Mason read a book he liked or hated or was moved by, he would buy another and underline words and sometimes whole passages. Then he gave them to me. We went to Paris after he read *Giovanni's Room*. It was the happiest time of my life. I love him still." Dr. Bernard began to weep. I reached out and touched his hand.

"Don't take only what life gives you, reach out and take what you want," he said.

We sat quietly in the room thick with memories and desire. Reading my own copy of *Giovanni's Room* a few days later lit a fire in me. The main character, David, a white American living in Paris, begins a passionate affair with an Italian bartender, Giovanni, but because David is ashamed and scared of his desire, his love for Giovanni destroys them both. I was determined to have no such regrets, no such fears. I was still young and thought anything was possible.

I was awake, but I was dreaming about Paris, reading Baldwin, planning a new life. I made a reservation on a flight to Paris. I gave Dr. Bernard one month's notice, he gave me his blessings and a gold pen. When I told Aunt Vic I wanted to go to Paris, she didn't laugh or ask me if I was crazy; she sat down on her sofa, leaned over, and peeled back the carpet. She counted eighteen twenty-dollar bills into my hand and promised to send me more if I needed money to come home.

"I wish *I* had the balls to do it." She hugged me hard.

"Aunt Vic, that's some salty talk."

My mother was still deep in her grief over losing my father. She let her sadness at my leaving roll over her like a fog.

"Child, I wish I could see you married, but I know that's a long ways off. You still restless." She stroked my hair and kissed my third eye.

"Aren't you glad I didn't marry Leo just to ease your mind?"

"He was too handsome to be a husband anyway," she said, trying to comfort me. I had already put him in a box and shoveled dirt on top.

I had saved three hundred dollars, and I figured after selling everything I couldn't carry to France I'd have about five hundred more. I watched ten French videos in fourteen days to prepare my ear for my new language. Four weeks later I had a ticket to Paris.

The day after I arrived in Paris a bomb was found on a train headed toward Lyon. I wondered if my new friend Delphine had noticed a plain package underneath a seat near her. Had she panicked? Did she call the conductor and save the lives of dozens of passengers and her own life as well?

In another country, reading the words "two men kissed"
makes it possible for me to kiss any lips my heart desires.
In another country, the sound of music breathes.

In another country, love means this moment, now.
It means remembering your mother's face
when you told her you were leaving,
your lover's smell on that last day.
Good-bye is so final,
say: til then.

I carry words around in my pocket, put them behind my eyelids, in my mind. I let words float in my mouth. I roll them around on my tongue, taste them until sounds slowly push out of my mouth. Each word is a poem.

parler . . . la verité . . . à minuit . . . regarde . . . une étoile . . . le nuage . . . fumée

This new language I am dreaming, I'm beginning to understand, is soft in my mouth like small satin pillows. These words are not hard to swallow.

Once upon a time, not so long ago and not far from now, there was a black girl in Paris . . . She is lying on her back on a hard little bed with her eyes closed dreaming in French . . . The long narrow room . . . a round window at the foot of the bed . . . All the familiar things are not. A door is not a door. *La porte.* Love is *l'amour,* not an open wound. When I wake up I'll leave this place and I'll find my way back again. I'll find a word and sing it like it's the last song I'll ever sing. Josephine and jazz were here. It is a brand-new world.

My name is Eden and I'm not afraid of anything anymore.

traveling companion

THERE ARE SEVEN rules for living, according to Indego Black-Smith. He was more than willing to tell me all of them if I would have another glass of Côte du Rhône with him at his favorite bar, at the foot of the Panthéon.

He was a familiar sight in Paris, but tourists still stopped to stare at Indego when he passed in the street. He was the blackest man I had ever seen, and he was the wisest and the most beautiful. His hair was long and white and sprayed out from under his black beret and over his thin shoulders like wild grass. His clean-shaven face was unlined, his large amber eyes were watery, dreamy. He was tall and lean, his movements birdlike, quick, animated. Sometimes I forgot that he was nearly forty years older than I was, as old as my father when he died. He took my arm at the elbow like a gentleman when we crossed the treacherous Paris streets, dodging Citröens, Mercedes Benzes, and Renaults. He kept hold of me as if I were a lost child who might run away if given half a chance. I took double steps to keep up with him. He exhausted me. We had developed a strange relationship, he and I, since our first meeting at the American Bookstore near the Seine. The black Frenchman told me where to find him.

"Excuse me. I'm looking for a writer. A black American," I said.

I said it again, louder, because the old man sitting behind the counter, his scrawny body swimming in an ugly green tweed suit, looked past me. He looked around if a mosquito was buzzing in his ear. His creased, leathery skin was the pale gray of unbaked dough left out too long. I could see I'd interrupted his lunch, and the ugly green suit was not pleased. Crumbs of English biscuits were sprinkled in his scraggly beard, but only French fell from his lips.

"Qu'est-ce que vous voulez?" he growled, mouth full of food.

I couldn't translate fast enough. After only two days in the city the French language was still slow to register in my mind. I could see that in his eyes I was a tourist. His contempt for me was as plain as the dirt on his collar. I wanted to smack him on the head with the thick hard-bound volume of Proust's *Remembrance of Things Past* shelved near his right shoulder, but just then a gaunt, greasy-haired villain with sharp yellow teeth appeared from behind a stack of books, looking as if he had stepped out of a Dickens novel. He was wearing a blue velvet blazer, a white ruffled shirt with a red paisley cravat at his neck, and worn blue jeans hugging his narrow hips. A middle-aged version of the old man.

"You're looking for Indego?"

I nodded.

"He's outside. They're not speaking today," he said with a clipped British accent, tilting his head toward the ugly green suit. His beady eyes licked me from head to toe.

"Merci beaucoup," I said, and turned to leave.

The old man gave the younger one a look to shrivel, kept eating his biscuit, then dropped his head to continue reading the book spread open in front of him. Before I could walk out the door a young blonde American girl stepped up behind me. She put a travel magazine on the counter next to the old man's plate of crumbs. The old man stared at her and only reluctantly accepted the large bill she handed him. He spoke to her in perfect American English.

"You don't have anything smaller, dear?" He gave me an evil grin as if he had played a joke on me. I was not amused. I hoped Indego would have better manners.

It was a gorgeous breezy early autumn day. The sky was bright blue and flowers were blooming everywhere, even between the stones in the sidewalk. Leaves seemed determined to stay on the trees. Indego was sitting on a bench several feet to the right of the bookstore, reading the *International Herald Tribune*. A pair of bifocals held together with bits of black tape perched on the end of his nose. He seemed oblivious to the clusters of noisy tourists shuffling around him, cameras weighing heavy on their necks.

"Mr. Black-Smith?"

"And you are?" He did not look up from his reading.

"Eden." I shifted my backpack from one shoulder to the other and lost hope that he would be any friendlier than the ugly green suit in the bookstore behind me. There must be other writers who would tell me things I needed to know, I thought.

"I see." His gaze absorbed me. "*Who* are you?" His sugar-coated eyes were distorted by the bifocals and looked like fish eyes swimming under glass. He made a rattling noise deep in his throat.

"I'm a writer too and I . . . I mean I want to be a writer . . ." Suddenly I started to lose my nerve. My backpack fell to the ground, but my eyes stayed locked on his.

"A soul sister." He focused on my face, then turned his ear toward me as if he remembered the sound of my voice. "Let's take a walk, soul sister." And just like that, I became his traveling companion and he became my teacher, my guide. He folded up the newspaper neatly, then stood up to stretch as if he had awaked from a dream. I picked up my backpack from the ground and followed him. Indego went inside the shop with the newspaper. I waited outside, reading the titles of dusty discounted books stacked in open boxes on either side of the entrance. Most of the titles were in French or German with bold black and red lettering on plain cream covers. I promised myself I would take classes in French as soon as I saved some money. I wanted to lose myself in the language. I wondered what it would be like to dream in French, to make love in French. Would my dreams be more vivid? Were French kisses more profound? I watched Indego through the window. He laughed with the ugly green suit, then moments later hurried outside empty-handed, adjusting his worn jacket and the cloth bag slung across his chest with papers peeking out. He was wearing a blue plaid shirt with frayed collar and cuffs under a gray V-neck sweater, a bright red plastic tie with blue fish swimming up toward his chin. His brown corduroy pants hung loose on his thin frame, a worn black belt with extra holes punched in it held them up. His shoes were scuffed brown leather boots that seemed to be held together with hope. He took my arm and guided me through unfamiliar alleys he said were shortcuts, pointing out his favorite bakery, the square where the open market was held on Tuesdays, the Hotel California where Langston Hughes stayed, the Presence Africaine bookstore where literary treasures in the window looked at us like eyes, and he promised to show me more. I wondered if he knew James Baldwin, but I didn't dare ask, or have the opportunity to ask much. Indego talked almost nonstop. I felt as if I were being led into a maze with no hope of remembering my way out and no way to mark the journey except by memory. My mind took high-speed snapshots of everything I saw, like an automatic camera that clicked every few seconds. I began to make maps of my experience. I could feel my inner landscape changing, my edges softening.

After we settled into the corner table in the window of his favorite café Indego ordered a bottle of Côte du Rhône, then began to plan our days together. He looked deep into my eyes and said I seemed so familiar to him.

"Langston sent you, didn't he?" He reached for my hand. I relaxed, smiled, took a sip of wine.

My journal entries became brief, breathless.
Night falls. I surrender. My lonely days are gone.

seven rules for living

1. Always be prepared for the best of times and the worst of times.

When Indego and I arrived at the café in Montmartre his friends weren't there. He ordered cheese omelettes for both of us. By the time he ordered two *express* his friends still hadn't shown up, and for a while he was worried because they had promised to pay for dinner. He ordered another glass of wine and I had another one too because it was cheaper than a Coke. In the three days I had been attached to him I had never seen Indego pay for a meal, it seemed to be the price one paid for his company. I was worried that he would ask me to pay this time. But Indego made friends with a Dutch couple at a nearby table. They were tourists on vacation in Paris for the first time. The husband was an art collector; the wife didn't speak much, she just looked at us suspiciously. Indego told the husband which galleries wouldn't cheat them, which restaurants served choice cuts of beef, where to listen to the most authentic jazz, the best places in the Marais to buy *pain au chocolat* and cheese. He described places only someone who knows the city could show them. He promised to take us all to the top of Samaritaine department store to see a spectacular 360-degree view of Paris. He told us that on the eleventh floor, on the open rooftop terrace, there was a century-old map of Paris landmarks painted on colorful Italian tiles that corresponded to the architectural structures in the distance. My map of the world was expanding. I drew a circle with Paris in the center and noted my discoveries in blue ink.

Before the check could arrive at our table the Dutch husband discreetly paid our bill. He announced that he would meet us the following morning for a guided tour of the *lle de la Cité*. The wife blinked at us and stuttered something in Dutch to the husband. The husband put his large hand on the top of his wife's head and patted her like a child who has interrupted an adult conversation.

"We'll meet at Place du Châtelet at the fountain, nine o'clock sharp." Indego winked at me and drained his third glass of wine. The rendezvous made me nervous. Hôtel de Ville was nearby. It was where Prime Minister Jacques Chirac held office as mayor of Paris and had recently been the site of a bombing that killed a female postal clerk and wounded eighteen others in the underground post office. At the beginning of September, Lebanese terrorists had given the French government an ultimatum to release three jailed suspected terrorists. When the deadline passed, bombs had been placed in crowded public areas with the intent to kill.

"Is it safe?" I asked. Indego hunched his shoulders.

"You can't stop living your life. Everybody is scared, but you can't let fear rule your life."

I took a deep breath. If I could outrun trouble in my dreams, why couldn't I avoid it with my eyes open too?

Four more bombs went off in the next six days, killing a total of eight people and wounding nearly two hundred. The police were granted new powers to detain and deport suspected terrorists, given free license to stop Arabs on sight. I was terrified but tried not to let it show. I made a mental note to stop having my mail sent to the American Express Office near the Place de l'Opéra and to make sure my passport was in the little zippered money belt I kept around my waist underneath my clothes at all times in case I was stopped and asked for identification. I was hopeful I'd have a more permanent address soon, especially if I could prove myself responsible to Indego and be allowed to stay in his apartment until he returned from a planned trip to Germany.

After the Dutch couple left the restaurant and we were alone again, Indego told me long stories that circled and wound around backward like the arms of a clock in a broken mirror. He mesmerized me with his life adventures. He was born in Texas to a family of musicians and studied the world, traveling from coast to coast on trains, on buses, and in broken-down automobiles. The smell of small roasted birds, squirrels, and rabbits on an open fire. Missing his mama, moonlit nights in the arms of pretty country girls, and words he strung together like the notes of his father's saxophone to the rhythm of a train moving across the Midwestern plains. His stories made me think about things I thought I'd forgotten. My father's apple-scented pipe, my mother's quilts, Aunt Victorine's copper-colored lipstick. I missed home. I didn't remember to be heartbroken, but I was reminded of the look on my mother's face when I told her I was leaving, at first surprise, then her face falling down defeated like a cake in an oven that's been opened too soon.

2. Never tell a woman you love her or she'll break your heart.

"I told my first wife I loved her and she ran off with my best friend and took my Spanish guitar and a signed first edition of Langston's first book of poetry, *The Weary Blues.* She could've taken my clothes, my records, and all my money, but that book meant the world to me, it was how I came to be a poet, chewing on those poems. I used to sing them. He was a genius and he was kind to me. Some people didn't like him because he was homosexual. What two men or three women do in their bed is no business of mine. Now, me myself, I prefer the smell, the taste, the sound of a woman under my bones. It ain't no better, ain't no worse."

Indego liked to tell stories, to hear the sound of his voice. He offered me a place to stay. He was going away for a month or two and he implied that if things worked out, I could stay in the apartment, look after things for him. After spending three nights in his bed alone I wondered if I was supposed to be sleeping with him in exchange for rent. He said nothing and neither did I. It was just a feeling. I got up and made the bed when I heard him in the bathroom clearing his throat, riffing like Betty Carter to Miles Davis's "Kind of Blue." The soft double bed was surrounded by stacks of jazz albums, which took up most of the tiny bedroom. I put water on to boil in the windowless, grease-gray kitchen the size of a closet, and put away the dishes from the night before. Indego kissed me on both cheeks as I passed him in the hall. We traded places. He made breakfast, strong black coffee, a slice of dry bread, and fruit, peeled, cut into small pieces, and carefully measured equally into two wooden bowls from Bali. I washed and dressed quickly in the bathroom painted like a corner of a pale blue sky with impressionistic clouds on the floor and ceiling. We ate in silence. After our morning meditation, *I eat his stories.* When he got started, Indego did not stop talking. At night I could hear him mumbling to himself until I fell into dreams.

In a rare moment of silence I took the opportunity to ask a question that had been burning in my mind since the day I met him.

"Do you know James Baldwin?"

"Jimmy? Yeah, I know Jimmy." He paused and laughed. "He was the life of any party he was at, and he never said a cross word to me. We was drinking buddies when he first got here. I used to call him Empty Pockets, but when he found out where the boys were I didn't see much of him. Brilliant. Say what you want about him, that bug-eyed brother could snatch a word and make it shout like it's been in church all day on a Sunday. His favorite word was 'love-you-man,' like he'd invented it. He said it like it was one word, 'love-you-man.' " Indego wiped at the corners of his mouth, delicately sipped from his cup, and looked past me, back to where he and Jimmy lived then.

"You could always count on Jimmy for a good story and a good laugh and a piece of change if he had it."

He was quiet again, stirring his spoon in the empty cup.

"Never tell a woman you love her, because she will break your heart. I told my third wife, and she burned all my clothes and used three of my best poems to wipe her behind. Love is the kind of word that can mess up a good thing.

Except when Jimmy said it, he said it plain, 'love-you-man,' and he meant it."

3. When you look at the world, try to see something new.

Indego was also a filmmaker, and I was flattered that he wanted me to star in his new film, *The Old Man's First Kiss from the Virgin*.

"You are so familiar to me. Have you ever been to Cairo?" His eyes hypnotized me. I leaned in when he drew his fingers in the air, beckoning me closer for a deep, throaty, wine-scented whisper.

"Have you ever had sex on an elephant?" I looked at him, and he was grinning at me as if he could tell I had not had sex of any kind in a long time. He tried to seduce me from the first take. I tried to pretend, to be a good actress, but all I felt was sentimental and tenderness when I kissed him. *His hand is my father's hand*.

"Why did you come to Paris?" I avoided his eyes.

"I had to kill somebody." He left his confession to smoke in the air.

"Why?" I had been sleeping in his bed for one week and that was the first time it occurred to me to wonder if he strangled girls in their sleep, chopped them to pieces, and boiled them in a soup. *His eyes are my father's eyes*.

"Because I loved my friend and I made the mistake of trying to save him. You can't save nobody but yourself. My friend tried to kill me, and I had to cut him loose. I didn't want either of us to go to jail for murder. He thought I was in love with his wife."

"Were you?"

"We'd seen each other naked was all. There was no love in that."

The camera rolled. We lay together in the sun on a yellow blanket surrounded by high grass in the Bois de Boulogne while one of three bearded German film students circled us with his eye to the camera. Indego rested his chin between my shoulders. I turned in the circle of his arms. His dark chocolate skin smelled like warm milk and peppermint.

"There may be snow on the mountain, but there's fire down below." He spoke his lines directly into the camera. Indego was trying hard to seduce me. His life was a beautiful poem and he wanted me to be in it. I closed my eyes and drifted into a green sea of grass.

I became Indego's traveling companion. He had been all over the world, and we traveled the same paths together when he told his stories. Italy, Morocco, Sweden, the women, the wine, the crocodiles.

> I looked into a bowl of water
> and saw reflected there
> an eye, a mouth, a heart, a bird
> I dived into the liquid air . . .

4. **Don't steal nothing you can't take and make your own. To thine own self be true. Know who you are.**

Elsa, a long-legged Swedish ex-model and part-time poet, Umi, a petite Japanese art student with big eyes and a tiny mouth, and I followed Indego blindly through the narrow crowded streets of the Marais to the Musée Picasso. Elsa paid for all of us from a fat roll of new French francs. Once we were inside the ornate villa Indego commanded us to sit and contemplate the works to absorb them. Elsa took copious notes. Umi and I giggled at the odd angles and shapes of the faces of Picasso's wives and lovers. We looked at them upside down, through squinty eyes, through a cardboard square the size of a postage stamp. Umi and I used lots of sign language to communicate because she spoke only French and Japanese. My French was so basic I could converse only with small children and animals. Indego told us about Picasso's love life and carried on a monologue about the African influence in Picasso's work.

"When Pablo first saw those African masks and fetishes he went wild. It was like he had jungle fever. You can see it in his portrait of Gertrude Stein. You can see it over there, in that one, and this one here . . ."

After the Picasso museum we sat in a park across the street, sharing food we had each brought. Umi had a couple of nori rolls cut in half and a can of lychee fruit in sweet syrup. Elsa had a mozzarella, basil, and tomato sandwich on french bread and two apples; I had a small cut of manchego cheese, a hard roll, and a bag of salted pistachio nuts. Indego had a knife to cut the food for us and a clean white handkerchief to spread across his lap to put his share on. He also produced several paper-covered toothpicks for us to take a stab at Umi's lychees.

At the Musée d'Orsay he directed our eyes to the sweeping architecture and the quality of light in the enormous, elegant space that was once a busy train station and now housed nineteenth-century Impressionist paintings, photography, sculpture, and decorative arts. Elsa and Umi were over-whelmed and tired. They said good-bye to Indego and me, kiss-ing the air beside our cheeks before walking away arm in arm toward the métro.

Indego and I went alone to the African and Oceanic mu-seum. He lectured to me on African history like a *griot,* a sto-ryteller whose responsibility it is to pass on the history of the tribe.

"When Europeans were still living in caves Africans had al-ready created rich kingdoms . . ."

"Know where you've been, but don't live in the past. Know where you're going, you need concrete goals even if they're short-term, but the most important thing is to know who you are. There are some West Indians living here who have com-pletely assimilated into French culture. Men and women who think and feel French. The only thing African about them is their color. It is true that there are no places here that keep a black person out, no, the French are not racist in that way. But there is a kind of condescension, a superiority, a patronizing attitude that comes through between most foreigners and the average French person. When the French colonized Caribbean and African countries they were as ruthless as the British, the only difference was that they were tolerant of those who adopted the French way of life. That is what makes one French—culture, language, and attitude. The French kept their former colonies as *départements,* which are like distant *ar-rondissements.* So technically your Martiniquan friend is as French as all persons born in France. There has been new leg-islation to limit access to citizenship because of the flood of new immigrants like the Haitians and Ethiopians. Don't be confused about who you are, this is one of the main keys to life."

5. Don't hurry love.

We lay together spoon-fashion on the sofa bed in Indego's living room to keep each other warm. The door to the bathroom was closed. On a large poster Manet's pale young Olympia lay naked watching over us, tempting, teasing as the black maid offered a bouquet. A dim yellow lamp burned on a bookshelf near our feet. The BBC world news report sounded distant and staticky. Deportations. Hijackings. Bombings. Protests. Strikes. The world outside was falling to pieces as I was falling to sleep. It was so cold in the room that I could see mist clouding the air when I breathed. The windowless room was lined with books from floor to ceiling. It felt like a kind of cave. The big soft bed I had slept in for two nights alone in the room down the hall was even colder, although thick Turkish carpets lined the walls, floor, and ceiling. Indego's bony legs wrapped around mine. I was annoyed that he kept shifting his body behind me, but I said nothing. I hoped he would settle down soon so I could get some sleep. I was tired from walking around museums all day. My head was full of images I wanted to dream about. Maps of places I wanted to go. Cézanne's colors, Picasso's shapes, ancient African deities, crown jewels sparkling against black velvet, hieroglyphic messages inside Egyptian tombs, rivers of broken glass.

Indego was wearing a blue cone-shaped flannel nightcap, a wheat-colored suit of long underwear that buttoned down the front, and a pair of thick black socks. I was wearing long underwear that matched his and two pairs of red wool socks and a green knit cap Indego gave me to keep my dreams to myself. I knew he wanted to make love, but he wanted me to make the first move. He spoke in metaphor and simile about the poetry of love, the passion and experience age brings to any union of love. I fell asleep with his breath warm on the back of my neck.

In my sleep I feel a slow hand searching between the top buttons on the front of my long johns. My breasts are sleeping and this hand wakes them up. The hand washes each breast like a hand washing a pear before a mouth bites into it. Fingers pluck at my nipples delicately as if they are grapes that do not want to be wine. The sting is sweet, the fingers strong. The hand makes a harvest of my body. My body opens, twists and turns slowly under the musty flannel covers, stirs under the hand washing my body, rising up to meet the promise it makes. Kisses bite and burn my flesh. My body takes the hand, the mouth, the face, the insistent loving and turns inside out, folds and unfolds, cracks open, spreads out like wings in a weightless sky. The other body rocks and stirs from behind. An unhurried, deep and infinite sinking into my body from midnight till morning. We sigh, open and close. I feel peaceful.

After making love we lay face to face. Indego's eyes shone like new copper pennies in the dark.

6. You must live, not just exist. *Il faut vivre et non pas seulement exister.*

Her laughter rattled the silver. Her girlish giggles shook the water in the crystal glasses. Her coy smile made the roses bloom in their winter vases.

One of Indego's long-ago girlfriends, Carmen, a rich Chilean woman in her sixties or seventies with jet black hair and a diamond ring on each of her manicured fingers saw us passing by La Coupole one afternoon and invited us to have dinner with her. There was a lonely look about her, but her too tight face seemed to shine when Indego looked at her. She was coy with him and tolerated me as a chaperone.

From table fifty-three on a clear day you could see the wings of Notre-Dame and the tip of the island on which it sits. It seemed as if I could see all of Paris that mattered from the wide sweeping windows of La Tour d'Argent. Princes and presidents, showgirls and actresses had dined here. It was one of the most expensive restaurants in the city and the reason soon became clear. The waiters were attentive without being intrusive. They were polite and complimented me when I tried to order in French. I was grateful for the flattery whether they meant it or not. I had been practicing speaking French every chance I got. The meal was dramatically presented, each plate a small Impressionist painting, each forkful made my mouth happy.

VOL AU VENT DE LA MER
PUFF OF WIND FROM THE SEA
a delicate golden pastry shell filled with a mixture of seafood in a rich, creamy sauce

Carmen had just come from her house in the Camargue region, where she rested and painted pictures of wild horses and the unspoiled landscape. "*La vie est belle*. Life is beautiful," she said, "if you live it right."

DÉGUSTATION DE POISSON GRILLÉ,
*grilled fish in a circle of buttered miniature carrots, tiny zucchini
and finger-length potatoes garnished with minced parsley*

"Remember when we drove together through the desert on the motorcycle? We watched a dozen sunrises in Morocco, flew over the Amazon in a tiny airplane, drank morning dew from roses in the gardens at Saratoga after a night at the races. Ah, that was living." Carmen pressed her hand to her heavy bosom. Indego nodded and smiled, remembering with her.

SOUFFLÉ CHAUD À LA MANDARINE,
*warm mandarin soufflé and a tray of miniature pastries,
mille-feuilles, fruit tarts, and pastel-frosted cakes*

I glanced at the bill and nearly choked to see that it was more than three thousand francs. I could have lived on that amount for a few months.

"We lived like youth, and money would last forever. I've nearly lost it all," she said, "but I have no regrets. I'm happiest to eat dessert first." Carmen fumbled in her silver tear-shaped purse for a credit card and lit another cigarette.

"*Hay que vivir y no sólo existir.* In any language, you must live, not simply exist. The French have this one thing right. This, my dear," she waved her hand around the blue and gold room, "is living." The meal was certainly the most beautiful and the most delicious I'd ever tasted. I understood Carmen and felt that I was living, and when I could, I'd always eat dessert first.

7. **Make your own rules and break every one of them. Every rule is meant to be broken.**

Indego took me to a small hotel on the boulevard St-Michel and paid for two nights. He said he had found a paying tenant to sublet his apartment for the next few months. He left the next morning with Carmen with the promise of a safari in Kenya and winter in the sun. I was not unhappy to be on my own again. Indego had moved us quickly through the city, and there were places I wanted to explore slowly and leisurely, but I had only two days to find a job or I would soon be sleeping on a park bench or trying to sell my clothes from a blanket in the métro.

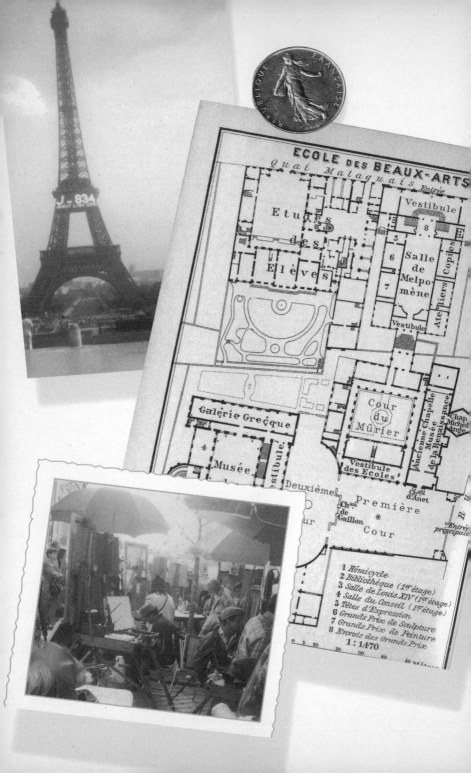

ECOLE DES BEAUX-ARTS

Quai Malaquais Entrée

Etudes
des
Elèves

Vestibule

8

Salle
de
Melpo-
mène

5

6

7

Ate liers Copies

Vestibule

Galérie Grecque

4

Musée

Vestibule

Cour
du
Mûrier

Ancienne Chapelle
du Musée
de la Renaissance

Chap
Michel
Ange

Chau
d'Anet

Vestibule
des Ecoles

Deuxième

Cour

Chau
de
Gaillon

Première

Cour

Entrée
principale

1 Hémicycle
2 Bibliothèque (1er étage)
3 Salle de Louis XIV (1er étage)
4 Salle du Conseil (1er étage)
5 Têtes d'Expression
6 Grands Prix de Sculpture
7 Grands Prix de Peinture
8 Envois des Grands Prix

1 : 1.470

0   5   10
    20   30
    40   50

50 Mètres

artist's model I: paris

I KNEW I COULDN'T STAY with Indego forever. I hadn't been able to contribute much to the household, and this was starting to cause tension between us. Even though Indego had paid for my hotel room for two nights, I wouldn't be able to afford to stay beyond his final generosity. But it was easy to move with so few possessions. There wasn't enough to weigh me down, and I was prepared to let go anything that tried. It was strange to say good-bye so easily, but Paris was having the effect on me of allowing me to believe that a good-bye wasn't gone. I realized that what I wanted most was to be alone for a while after all. My mind was crowded with Indego's thoughts, his impressions, his ideas, his way of looking at things. I wanted a place to be with myself, to absorb all the richness of Paris quietly, to explore and discover my own inner mysteries. What I desired most was a room of my own in which to wrestle with the choices barely becoming visible to me. Reality was a hammer falling on my head, empty pockets couldn't take me far. After Indego left with Carmen for Kenya, I called Delphine, who told me about a friend of hers who sometimes modeled for artists at the Ecole des Beaux Arts and the Académie Julien. She said that sometimes individual artists put up ads for models on the notice boards. She went with me the next day to the Ecole des Beaux Arts, where we were told curtly in rapid French that new regulations required artist models to have a carte de séjour, an official work permit issued by the French government. The woman told us that working papers were difficult to get since stricter immigration rules were being enforced. Delphine translated for me, and we left disappointed.

"*Officially* the new laws were designed to contain the new wave of terrorism, *unofficially* they were created to keep out new immigrants. There are still many fascists in our society." Delphine met me each week and usually treated me to hot chocolate or coffee in one of various cafés around the Latin Quarter, where she practiced her English and corrected my French. She listened to my adventures with Indego and laughed imagining me trying to figure out which forks to use at my elegant dinner at La Tour d'Argent. She was pleased I had seen so much of the city and to hear that I was no longer afraid to try out my French. Often listeners would ask me to repeat my slow patch of words and phrases, but I was beginning to understand and make myself understood in the métro asking for tickets, asking strangers for the time, requesting a *croque monsieur* or a fried cheese sandwich at a café.

"You have to be willing to make mistakes to learn," Delphine said.

She and I discussed a plan to help me find employment, but she warned me to be careful.

"If you are caught working without a permit you could be deported," she said as we both watched tourists walk by snapping photographs of everything, including us. It was odd to think that my picture would be in a stranger's book of memories. *What is that? The Eiffel Tower. Who is this? A black girl in Paris.*

Delphine was not the kind of girl to buy used clothes, but she told me about the flea market at the American Church and the huge *marché aux puces,* an enormous outdoor flea market with clothes, from vintage lace lingerie to thick-soled Czech shoes, antiques, rugs, paintings, African masks and Turkish tea glasses, and all manner of household items. It was held outside métro de Montreuil. The *marché aux puces* was where I found a black beaded blouse and green silk skirt with faint watermarks at the waist and an oversized man's winter coat with holes in the lining for forty-five francs. The coat was not very stylish, but it kept me warm, and no one could see the lining if I kept it buttoned.

"My mother says you have to be careful about wearing used clothes. There could be something left on them," I said.

"Like what?"

"Death or sickness could be clinging to them. I always wash them with salt before I wear them. Then I have to sleep with them under my bed."

"Why would you do that?" She laughed.

"If I have good dreams I can keep them."

Delphine looked puzzled.

"My mother believes that if you wear a dead person's clothes their spirit might still be in them, and with used clothes you don't know where they come from."

Delphine said that I looked very French in my new old clothes. After a good night's rest I wore them to the dinner party Delphine invited me to. Delphine was dressed as if she were going to a tea party when she met me after her classes at Science Po.

She was an upper-level student, already preparing for her life as lawyer for an international corporation. I thought her English was good. She also spoke Italian and some Japanese.

She told me about her family. They had been *pieds-noirs*, French citizens who worked abroad in Algeria, Morocco, Africa, the former French colonies. Her parents, she said, were nostalgic for the time they spent in Africa.

"They remember it being a little France with dusty, picturesque villages and veiled women, camels and Muslim men in big dresses and head wraps. My parents live in a romantic colonial past. When the war began we had to return to France. I was born in Algeria, so I guess I am a little bit African too."

That was the only thing African about her, I thought. To me she seemed absolutely French.

Indego had told me about the seven-year war for Algerian

independence, which was suppressed ruthlessly and brutally by the French, who used murder and torture to control the population. The French also advanced as scientific fact theories that Algerians were born liars, thieves, and criminals. To my amazement these theories were taught in French universities for more than twenty years.

"My parents live in the country now and seem happy to grow olives and drink wine." I wondered if they had nightmares, if they still heard screams in the night.

"Tonight my friends would like to meet you. They are mostly artists like you."

I bought an inexpensive bottle of wine, a Beaujolais Village Delphine picked out. Delphine carried two baguettes, two dinner plates, and place settings for each of us because the host kept only one set of dishes. Everyone was bringing something. I was looking forward to meeting other students. It was hard to meet people without speaking their language, and I knew that it was unusual and lucky for me to have made a French friend on my first day in Paris. I was appreciative of the time she was taking to aquaint me with her city, her language and customs. We took the métro to a part of Paris unfamiliar to me and walked several blocks down a quiet tree-lined street to an apartment building near Les Invalides. Delphine tapped out the door's entry code, and we entered a brightly lit foyer. A girl was standing at the far, inner door. Her large, broad face was expressionless when she saw us.

"Is this your American friend?" the girl asked, tossing her two dark braids over her shoulder. She looked like a sad character in a children's picture book. Céleste was tall with handsome features. She wore a white blouse, short black skirt, and red-and-white striped knee socks. Her shoes were black patent leather loafers. She kissed Delphine on each cheek, and as I was about to extend my hand to shake hers, she kissed me— only once because I mistook her coming toward me—and we ended up in an awkward American hug. We giggled about international greetings, men kissing on the lips, rubbing noses, and formal bows as we walked up four flights. The door to Delphine's friend's apartment was open. Inside were two young men who looked like teenagers, laughing and smoking at a small table in the center of the tiny room. Another—Manuel, a sleepy-eyed Italian—lay on a small bed strumming a guitar. Pierre, a gaunt young man with long greasy hair and a scar on his face, sat at the table next to our host, Emil, a pale red-haired boy with a neatly groomed red beard. They each stood and greeted us with kisses. In heavily accented English they said that they were pleased to meet me. They laughed each time they said a phrase in English, as if they had practiced their lines and were surprised they remembered anything at all. They were good-natured, and the apartment was warm and smelled like spaghetti sauce. I was starving, but we did not eat for another hour. We drank wine, smoked cigarettes, and nibbled on bread, cheese, and olives until our red-haired host stood up and made a toast to me, their honored American guest. I blushed and said, *"Milles mercis, vous êtes très gentils,"* and hoped that translated into "Many thanks, you are very kind," just as I had practiced with Delphine. I looked at her, and she winked as if I had done fine. I looked around the tiny room as the conversation turned to politics in polite measured English. While they argued I got up and looked around the apartment. The room was painted a deep forest green. Dozens of sketches were taped to the wall at the far end of the room. A small bed that functioned as a sofa was pushed against a wall and covered with an Indian print bedspread. The kitchen was a tiny stove, a deep double sink, and a tiny refrigerator. A large bookcase was filled with books and sketchpads, watercolors, and boxes of pastels, jars of brushes. Tall French doors opened onto a tiny balcony, where I found a dark-skinned young man with a red silk scarf knotted around his neck sitting and smoking a cigarette. I hadn't noticed him before.

"Bon soir," I said, although my first impulse was to speak to him in English. He looked like one of the brothers back home, but when he spoke his accent was clearly French.

"You are Delphine's American friend. *Enchanté.* I am Sidi." He tossed the cigarette over the balcony. "I'm sorry to miss the chance to speak with you. Another time," he said and stood up abruptly. He went back in the main room, and the conversation stopped. I came in behind him, and he kissed us all twice in turn and said he was sorry he couldn't stay. Emil was the only one he didn't kiss. Sidi and Pierre left, slamming the door behind them. I found out from Delphine later that Sidi was from Senegal and that he and Emil had been lovers for the past year. After a small pause in the conversation Emil shouted, *"À table,"* "Let's eat," and the mood became lighter. Sitting wedged between Delphine and Manuel, I tried to catch as much of the conversation as I could. They called Emil "Little Marcel," explaining to me that he was developing a collection of eccentricities much like his favorite author, Marcel Proust, who had slept all day and lived in a sealed, darkened apartment and died before he was truly appreciated. Emil felt misunderstood and underappreciated and seemed to believe he was destined for greatness after his death, which he predicted would occur before he was thirty.

After several drinks Delphine's friends began to speak to each other freely in French. I couldn't follow but smiled a lot as if I understood their jokes. From time to time Delphine would ask me if I understood something and translate for me, but after a while she seemed to forget about me. I understood when they began to talk about the students being on strike and the police harassing students. They were angry and intolerant of extreme right-wing politicians like Le Pen attempting to introduce racist legislation.

After the dinner of green salad, dressed with crushed garlic, olive oil, and lemon juice, a plate of pasta with a plain red sauce, a chunk of blue cheese, and the bread Delphine had bought, Emil made the strongest black coffee I'd ever had and served it with tiny wedges of a delicious apricot tart Céleste had brought. Emil pulled a large cardboard box from underneath the bed. It was filled with art supplies, tape, eight-by-ten sheets of thick white paper, scissors, cans of spray paint, and small X-acto knives. Someone passed me a lumpy cigarette. By the smell I guessed it was stuffed with marijuana or hashish. I passed it on but took another glass of wine. They began to make stencils of body outlines like ones found at crime scenes and wrote slogans to go along with them. That was only part of the night's work. Soon they would go out and use the stencils to spray paint slogans onto walls in the Latin Quarter and the Marais, striking a blow for the students. Delphine said it was too dangerous for me to go out with them because if I were caught I could be deported. She kissed me three times on my cheeks and gave me a piece of paper with the names of art schools where I might have luck looking for employment.

I went alone to the Académie Julien, where a thin, pleasant-faced young woman wearing a black-and-white striped dress and with green-streaked hair said she was sorry she couldn't help me. She slowly and patiently explained to me in halting English the new rules for hiring artists' models. She shrugged her shoulders and directed me to the notice board at the end of the hall. I thanked her and headed for it. There was a tiny notice tacked at the bottom of the board, the only one in English:

Artist seeks models to pose for painting.
No experience necessary. 100 francs per hour.

A number was listed with hours to call.

That afternoon I found myself in the Marais, the old Jewish quarter, a crowded place of narrow, winding streets, rich, spicy smells, thick incense, and dust. Old men in black fingered their beards, Russian and Yiddish phrases competed with the sound of balalaikas and opera music floating from open windows and shop doors. I felt as if I'd wandered into another century.

When I was in college I was asked by my art history professor if I wanted to make extra money modeling for an evening art class. One of the regular models had not shown up and they were desperate. I said yes, and when the realization sank in that I would be nude in a room full of strangers I felt the blood rush to my face in embarrassment. I arrived early for the first class and walked around the cold, empty room, pacing among the bare easels randomly placed across the paint-splattered floor. The professor arrived soon after I did and put me immediately at ease.

"Pretend that you are a bowl of fruit. That's how they'll see you, as an object, lines, curves. You will be a mystery for them to figure out on paper. Did you ever play the game statue as a kid? Just pretend that you're playing statue. When I say 'change' pretend you're another statue."

His instructions were invaluable. I went into the bathroom down the hall, took off my clothes, and put on a thin yellow bathrobe. When I returned the classroom was filled with about a dozen students, mostly male, joking with each other, noisily setting up large drawing pads on the easels. The professor introduced me to the class, thanked me for helping them out, and then asked me to step up on a raised carpeted platform. There was a small brown sofa on it, in front of a bank of high windows. I took off my robe and became a body, an art exercise, a statue. The professor played Bach on a cassette player and lit a stick of sandalwood incense, which relaxed me a little. It was a two-hour class. The professor walked around the room commenting on the drawings and mostly keeping his eyes off me, thankfully.

My first task was to get the students warmed up by creating a series of five poses, which I was to hold for no longer than a minute each. I made up a dance in my mind and froze each step when I heard the professor's voice ring out *Change*. Arms raised as if holding an Olympic torch in the air. *Change*. Arm swung back as if about to let go of a bowling ball down a lane. *Change*. A hunter with bow and arrow. *Change*. Kneeling on the carpeted platform with my head back and my hands covering my crotch. Next I held two poses for fifteen minutes. A hula dancer in mid-hula. *Change*. A devout nun in prayer. *Break*. It was harder to hold the longer poses, but I would breathe and imagine myself in Paris in a studio full of young Gauguins, Manets, and Beardens. Usually my mind wandered over thousands of little thoughts. New names for the color of the sky . . . the butterfly dishes on my mother's breakfast table . . . a birthday present for my father . . . reviewing the American history exam I failed . . . the sound of my heartbeat when I caught the eyes of a girl with braids concentrating on my bare breasts . . . After the first break I was allowed to choose a pose I could hold for thirty to forty-five minutes. The professor suggested that I use the sofa in some way. I posed, like the woman in the classical painting the *Lady and Maid,* but I was the lady. I lay on the backless sofa and pretended I was waiting for someone to peel me a grape. It was a vulnerable position. At first I thought I could feel their hands on my skin, but I soon left my body. I discovered that I could read in this position and would often bring books to read as I lay on the sheet-draped sofa. I almost forgot I was lying naked in a room of strangers who stared at my body until the teacher called out, "Break." I quickly got over the embarrassment of being naked, because no one ever referred to it. Sometimes the professor would come near me and point with a thin wooden pointer, bringing to the students' attention the line of a muscle in my leg or a shaded area beneath my breasts.

He was careful never to touch me or make me self-conscious. I was beginning to feel like an exhibitionist. After a few weeks of modeling I wanted to be naked all the time. On break I would stroll absentmindedly out into the hallway and drink from the water fountain, shocking the maintenance staff or students from other classes waiting for the elevator. The sketches I saw of myself made me feel good about my body. My handful of breasts, soft belly, and big thighs were sensuous lines in the eyes of the artists. Many of the students made flattering likenesses of me. I was disappointed that the artists hardly ever put details in my face although they captured the density and curl of my pubic hairs, the exact shape of my hardened nipples, and weight of my breasts against gravity. The professor complimented me on my concentration, creative poses, and ability to be as still as a statue for so long. My muscles ached for hours afterward. Suffering through those first awkward days in that incense-filled classroom had prepared me for my first modeling job in Paris, I hoped.

It was an adventure searching for the crumbling apartment building on the gloomy back streets. After passing the small street twice because it was not marked I was finally directed to an unnumbered doorway by a heavy-set woman smoking a cigar. She leaned against the wall of an alley wearing a bloody butcher's apron and blood-splattered gray rubber boots. Locked mailboxes lined the dark entryway. Across the courtyard I found the number the artist had given me over the phone. The elevator looked like one of the first ever built. I closed the black grill gate of the tiny two-person cage and rode to the fifth floor. It was dark on the landing, and I groped along the wall for the light switch. When I found 5C I knocked three times. I yawned and checked my watch. I was late, but I still hadn't gotten used to getting up at six o'clock in the morning. I heard several locks sliding open and a chain being dragged sluggishly across its track.

When the door opened I thought I'd gotten the wrong flat. The man at the door looked more like a medical doctor than an artist. Average height, slightly balding with white hair framing his large ruddy face, and a snow white beard and neatly trimmed moustache. Faded gray eyes looked at me from behind thick round tortoise-shell eyeglasses. He wore a white shirt, gold silk tie, brown wool vest, and matching cuffed pants under a white lab coat with the sleeves rolled up to his elbows. His face was kind, but his faded gray eyes were distant and his moustached mouth sagged as if he was grieving. He bowed stiffly from the waist, his arm outstretched to guide me inside.

"Entrez. Entrez," he said brusquely, looking at a thick gold watch on his wrist.

"Monsieur Deschamps?"

"Oui, oui. Entrez, mademoiselle," he said. "I am the artist. I am Henri."

I was surprised, but relief swept my face. Delphine had been worried that he might be a pervert. He looked harmless enough. He was so serious. He looked at me like a surgeon preparing for an important operation.

When I stepped inside the apartment I could see that it was small and very messy. It smelled of oil paint, stale cigarettes, turpentine, garlic, and cat piss. A thin black cat sitting on the windowsill was lapping at a crusted saucer of food surrounded by an army of ants. Newspaper was strewn over the floor, several easels with colorful painted portraits in various stages lined the walls. A wide single window looked out over hundreds of rooftops and an enormous pale silvery blue sky.

"We agree on the telephone. I pay you one hundred twenty francs for one hour. Please remove your clothes." He pointed to a gaily painted Japanese silk screen that barely reached my shoulders. I eyed the small cot covered with a ragged wool blanket. I bent down behind the screen and stripped, folding each piece of my clothing carefully and slowly. I could hear Henri moving around on the other side.

"Come out. Please do not be nervous. I am artist," Henri tried to reassure me.

I stepped from behind the screen onto the dirty newspapers, holding my hands in front of my body like a shield. The room was cool, and my body shivered as my naked thighs made contact with the chilly seat of the low stool he had wiped with the dirty rag in his hand. He draped a cleaner-looking towel on the stool.

"Sit. Cross your legs. Hold this please."

He handed me a large gray, glassy-eyed fish by the tail. It was cold and slippery, and I promptly dropped it onto the floor. The cat pounced on it. Henri kicked the cat hard in its ribs, and it screeched as it went flying across the room.

He frowned and held the fish out to me again, waiting for me to take it. I thought about my last fifty francs, in the bottom of my left shoe, and how hungry and cold I would be the next day if I couldn't pay my hotel bill. I took the fish from Henri's short, stubby fingers and held it by its tail away from my body.

The cat pawed at it for the next two hours, occasionally licking fish blood from between my toes. The cat's rough tongue tickled, but its warmth spread up my legs, and I tried to imagine that I was sitting in the sun getting a tan.

Henri sat in a white wicker chair before a large drawing pad. He sketched me from several different angles. As Henri drew my features I held on to the thought that the 240 francs he gave me would mean at least two more days of food in my stomach. The cat licked my ankles and purred contently. Henri coughed, then lit an unfiltered Gauloise cigarette, which dangled out of the side of his mouth as he worked. I could be in the basement of the Dimple Mansion, I thought, smiling inside; I could be wishing I was here. I soon forgot I wasn't wearing any clothes and relaxed enough to fantasize about drinking champagne with James Baldwin on Boulevard St-Germain at Café de Flore, celebrating the publication of my first book.

"How do you handle your fame, Mr. Baldwin?" I would ask him.

"You get used to it," he would say.

He would tell stories and I would listen, laugh, and wait for his secrets.

Sometimes I could hardly believe that I was breathing the same air, walking the same streets as he did.

The next time I came to Henri's apartment I knocked, and when he let me in he didn't even speak. I went behind the screen, undressed, and sat holding a dead fish while the cat kissed my feet for an hour. *Rest.* I wrapped the towel around myself and stood looking out the window. It was raining. Cold, wet, and gray.

"You're so serious," I said.

"I can tell jokes," he said, coming to stand beside me at the window.

"What kind of jokes?"

"Offensive ones."

I gave him a questioning look.

"Do not worry, they are not about blacks or women. They concern Jews. I know some very good jokes about the Holocaust." We kept looking out the window in silence. I looked for numbers on his arms, but there were none.

"I was not there, but I am a survivor. I drowned just the same," he said sadly. After that we told each other stories about our lives, and from time to time he smiled, showing a row of stained, crooked teeth. He taught himself to paint by going to the Louvre. He said he would steal the shape of a head from Goya, the shadow on a table from Vermeer, the color of light between the trees from Van Gogh.

Henri only once commented on my physical appearance.

"Your mouth is like a secret that promises to be unforgettable." He said it in a flat, distant voice, the only trace of emotion in his wistful eyes.

"I like mystery," he said. "I want to tell a story in the painting, one without a clear ending." After I spent a few days with Henri, he became beautiful to me. Listening to his stories I could see that he was permanently wounded. Alone in the world. Guilty for not dying in the war like almost everyone else he loved. In his stories he traveled at night, crawling across dry, bitter fields, followed by children and old women, until they found safety. He saved dozens, but he couldn't save a single one of his five sisters or his bedridden mother. He admitted that his experiences could have left him with a hard heart. After the second morning I sat for him, Henri started putting an extra fifty francs in the small white envelope he slipped into my pocket at the end of the session, and when I left he would kiss me once on my cheek.

Things we lost. Things we found. Things we both needed.

Henri was shocked to learn I had not yet been to the Louvre. I told him I thought it was expensive to enter. Henri said it was free on Sunday, and he ordered me to go. I took a bus to rue de Rivoli. I approached the massive building, and as I walked toward it I felt as small as a grain of sand on a beach. I was overwhelmed by its scale.

"You American?" I heard a man's voice behind me as I approached one of several entrances to the museum.

I nodded, embarrassed.

The voice came from an American tourist with a Southern drawl. He punched me lightly on the arm. "That's where they keep the Mona Lisa, huh?"

"There's a lot more than the Mona Lisa in there," I said, and quickly moved away from the tall man in the yellow plastic poncho and Western boots, trying to get as far away from the ugly American as possible.

I opened my bag to let the guard search it, then entered the palace of stolen treasures. As they stole my ancestors from

Africa, stole their language, erased their history and their names, they had stolen crucifixes from European churches, jewels from Chinese dynasties, tombs from Egyptian deserts. In the U.S. there was a movement to recover the bones of ethnic people from all over the world so they could have a proper burial. I wondered if or when France would give up its African bones. I wandered the marble hallways and arena-sized galleries for hours. Time was altered when I stared at paintings so rich with detail that I felt as if I could walk right into the dense woods, the intimate rooms, the dramatic battlefields and grand weddings. When I caught sight of the loud American in the yellow poncho I walked faster into the next room to escape him and began to search for an exit. The fresh air was like wine to me. I sat on a park bench and let all the colors and shapes fit themselves onto a map, into my mind.

It was a Wednesday if I remember correctly. I was on a bus near Montparnasse when I heard the distinct wail of French police sirens and the already heavy traffic came to a halt. Wednesday, the school children were out and the streets were busy with shoppers. It was late in the afternoon, around five-thirty, and the bus had stopped in front of a popular movie theater with bright posters advertising the features playing inside. People on the bus began to grumble about getting home. I did not have an appointment, no one was waiting for me, and my room was cold, so I was content to watch the streets filled with cars and hurrying people. A woman got on the bus and said that a bomb had gone off a few blocks away. The story rippled down the aisle.

The police would be checking for papers. A few people got off to walk. I was afraid the police might check for my papers, and I remembered I'd left my passport at the hotel. The bus took thirty minutes to travel five blocks. The next morning at a café I saw a discarded *International Herald Tribune*. Witnesses to the bombing reported seeing a black BMW with two men inside drive slowly down the street. The man on the passenger side got out in front of Tati, a discount department store on the rue de Rennes, and put a package in an open trash barrel, then got back in the car. A few seconds later there was a huge explosion that left five dead and fifty-three wounded. Several of the bodies were dismembered by the blast. It was the fifth bomb in ten days. Some thought the bombing was the work of Lebanese terrorists trying to obtain the release of three of their imprisoned comrades. Others interviewed believed the bombing was to protest the heavy French presence in the Middle East.

That night I went to the movies in the Latin Quarter with Delphine. Armed guards in the cinema's lobby searched our bags and patted us down for weapons. An older French woman in line in front of us was irate and refused the body search. She walked away, cursing the guards. Delphine and I sat in the front row. Gable was kissing Lombard when the bomb exploded. The cinema shook and the lights dimmed for blocks around. When the smoke cleared we could see piles of broken glass and bits of clothing and flesh stuck to the interior walls of the building. A spray of blood had changed the color of my dress. Body parts were melted to the floor like candle wax. An arm bent at the elbow, a misshapen finger pulled by the root from a hand. The last thing I remember before waking up was the sound of a woman screaming. I drew a map of places to avoid during times of war.

When I arrived at Henri's on that last day, his belongings were sitting in the hallway. He had been evicted. He was going to Provence to live with one of his former students who had prospered and owned a restaurant and hotel in a small village near Grasse. Henri suggested I pose for his friend Jean-Paul, who had organized a salon of amateur painters in his home. He gave me a folded piece of paper with a name and phone number on it.

"Jean-Paul is my good friend. He will take care of you. He can pay you more. You are an excellent subject, but I can no longer pay for your services." Nor could he pay the landlord, which meant I couldn't pay mine either. Henri kissed me three times and pressed a fifty-franc bill into the palm of my hand. I reached over and pressed my lips to his scratchy cheek and watched him turn the color of a beet.

They look at me as if I am a banquet and they are hungry mouths. My face a bowl of strawberries, my mouth a slice of melon, my breasts tender rounds of roast pork, my waist a curve of mango, my thighs crusty loaves of bread, my arms slender glasses of amber liqueur. They do not touch me, but I feel their eyes tear at my flesh. I like the way it feels.

Jean-Paul Valba's Salon des Artistes was a group of figurative painters that met twice a week in his bare, elegant apartment near the Eiffel Tower. Jean-Paul was a burly, gregarious

Belgian painter who wore heavy sweaters over his portly body, leather gloves with the fingers cut out on his tough, paint-stained hands, and a wool scarf wrapped around his thick neck. The apartment was cold and damp. Its pale green walls were hung with framed prints of Ingrès. *Women in the Turkish Bath, Odalisque* . . . this was the style in which they painted. Romantic, lush images of nude women in ancient and timeless settings. After the first night Jean-Paul asked me if I was available for at least two hours each afternoon for the following week.

After standing naked for fifteen minutes next to the drafty window, I wondered if I could last a week before I turned into a cold stone statue. It was so cold my skin felt permanently dimpled with goose bumps.

The artists greeted me warmly on that first day. There were three others besides Jean-Paul. Nasir, an unsmiling middle-aged Egyptian architect with hairy hands and bold brush strokes, who wore blue jeans and pastel polo shirts under a dirty workman's jacket. His gaze was direct and his handshake crushing. Charlotte was a handsome woman with long limbs and a square ruddy face. She was constantly brushing her long brown hair away from her face with the pointed end of her paintbrush. Her eyes were tentative and stayed away from my face. She wore a paint-splattered smock over a man's white shirt and riding pants. Malik was an awkward young man in his early twenties with oily olive skin, curly black hair, and large mournful eyes with dark circles underneath them, which made him look as if he hadn't slept in days. His blue shirt and khaki pants were always neatly pressed. His shoes, though, were well worn and had dirty white laces in them. He was nervous, and his painting was not as precise or as polished as the others', but it was more interesting. The others were always gentle in their criticisms of his work. I never once saw him smile, and he hardly spoke. His eyes were the hungriest.

For hours I stood near the window, twisting and turning my body in the perfect Paris light. At the end of the session Jean-Paul paid me and whispered that many artists fall in love with their models.

"We are no different," he said waving his hand around the room, but by then I was dressed and the eyes that had devoured me for hours were tired and no longer hungry.

One evening I saw Malik walking along boulevard St-Michel near the Seine, his head bent as if he was deep in thought. I called to him, and for the first time I saw him smile. We walked down the stairs to the stone beach and sat on a bench under a tree next to the Seine. For a while we just looked at the tourists crossing the Pont Louis-Philippe. I was uncomfortable with the silence, and I asked him where he was from. In halting English, as if he had waited all his life to speak to me, he said he was Muslim, that his parents had come to Paris from Algeria during World War I. His father was a construction worker. He and his family, friends, and neighbors all had suffered daily humiliations in their new home. Called dirty, stopped regularly by police and checked for drugs, turned down for jobs on the telephone when the interviewer asked his name. Both the Algerians and the French had lost many lives during the eight-year Algerian struggle for independence. His father served in the French army and later worked as a laborer in France. Malik was born in France and was technically

French, but in his heart, he said, "I am African like you." He gave me a small sketch he had made of me in which I was clothed in a long white dress and a veil made of stars.

One night it rained as I was on my way to Jean-Paul's. I arrived soaked to my skin. I dried off in the big marble bathroom and by my first break was still shivering so hard that Charlotte made me lie down on the sofa and covered me with a thick blanket and threw over that a musty Turkish rug. She brought me a cup of tea while the men smoked in the far corner of the room, discussing their work. The next night, even though I was coughing and had a fever, I went back to the salon because I needed the money. At the end of the session Charlotte took me home with her, where I stayed for several days recovering with the help of antibiotics prescribed by a friend of hers, a doctor at the American Hospital.

Charlotte was a Rockefeller. I found out by reading the stack of unanswered mail on her desk. Most of it was addressed to Rosie, which is what she said her family called her. I knew that even then. Charlotte made promises I knew she couldn't keep, but she was so kind to me. *Forever. Always. Unconditional.*

"I will teach you how to act as if you own plantations and have servants to draw your bath. I will dress you in style. Teach you how to choose wine and a china pattern." She said that was all I would need to know, but it wasn't. I didn't know how long I could keep pretending to be Rockefeller's niece.

Charlotte, I discovered, had a lot of projects, and I was her latest one. She had seen Josephine Baker in *Princess Tam Tam* too many times. She was trying to transform me into a black Rockefeller, and she was failing miserably. There were too many rules and restrictions in the life she was planning for me. This was not the kind of freedom I came to Paris for.

In the afternoons Charlotte would pour tea as if she were the Princess of Wales. She showed me slides of paintings and photographs and tested me on the biographies and techniques and periods of her favorites.

how to look at art

With your head. With your heart. From a distance. With your eyes shut tight. With your eyes wide open.

Look at the piece for a long time, close up and from a distance. Close your eyes and try to see the piece in your mind. What do you remember when it's gone? What details do you notice when you open your eyes? Is the piece the same? Are you the same?

All of her favorite artists were men. They were the best painters, she said. I tried to protest once, but she shushed me. Sometimes she would slip in a few slides of her own paintings and practically glow in the dark when I said that these were my favorites. They were. She used bright colors and painted landscapes of bodies in mythical scenes that made me feel as if they were places I could live. She kept up a stream of dialogue.

"It was very difficult for me to make friends with the French at first. Of course I did not speak French very well, and I was in the beginning too American. I didn't care. I don't much care for the company of women, with the exception of you."

She wanted to be the center of attention, so when she had parties she invited mostly men.

"I felt I had to sleep with men to learn about them. If I made love to a man I wanted him to know more than me. So my first lovers were much older. I hoped that they would tell me secrets. Most men told me lies, but pretty ones because I was young and had a nice figure once. Oh, my face was never pretty, I knew this, but my body opened bedroom doors."

When I met her she was old to me and her face was cut with lines, but her black eyes were bright when she told me stories. She was still handsome and had the body of a much younger woman. From behind she could have passed for forty, although she was well into her seventies. She wore tight black stretch pants and crisp white shirts buttoned up to the neck and a string of pearls.

Charlotte had married into the Rockefeller family and was rich in name only. After her husband died she came to Paris to be a painter, but there were so many better than she. She painted to amuse herself. She raced cars. Raised orchids and started a school for pet massage. When she was younger she specialized in partying on her monthly allowance from the trust fund left to her by her husband.

She knew I wanted to be a writer. "Write something happy, something gay. Your life is very interesting, but the sorrows of the poor angry blacks, my dear, that has been done."

I was angry and insulted. She didn't seem to notice when I turned away from her and began to gather the few things I had brought with me.

"Consider Baldwin." She laughed softly. "Paris was a relief for him. He didn't have 'colored only' signs to deal with, there weren't places off limits to him because of his color. He could relax here. I don't believe he was as angry as he seemed. But he was so articulate about his anger. He used words I'd have to look up in the dictionary, and he spoke so fast at times I couldn't keep up. He was preachy and very proper as if he were in church giving a sermon to the unconverted. He didn't act as if he were preaching to the choir, oh no. Oh, he made me want to burn down my father's house and dance around the flames."

Charlotte Rockefeller was not crazy, she was just plain ignorant and out of touch with reality. I stopped packing, and when I turned around she was painting her toenails burgundy.

"You met him?"

"We were at the same parties from time to time. I liked him right away, but he preached to me when I had done all I could for causes like civil rights. I sent them lots of my dead husband's money."

The more she drank from the bottle of sherry on the table beside the bed I had slept in, the more she talked. Before she fell asleep she told me there was more than one way to love a woman.

How to Love a Woman
1. With your head
2. With your heart
3. From a distance
4. With your eyes shut tight
5. With your eyes wide open

The things I learned about love . . .

Charlotte wanted to make me her pet, but men too have wanted that, and there is no love in that kind of relationship, in which one is always giving and the other always taking. Each day I discovered secret routes that led to places I never knew existed on the surface of the earth. I was greedy for experience, to learn how to get there and how to find a way to stay. Grass wasn't growing under my feet, and morning wouldn't find me in Rockefeller's house.

caisse nationale des monuments historiques et des sites

SAINTE CHAPELLE
entrée
PLEIN TARIF

VALABLE LE 11/08/1986
VENDU LE 11/08/1987 A 15h49
CAISSE No 23   0801
ticket à conserver en cas de contrôle

32F

47238012421

carte
STP ORANGE

Nom

Prénom   SPEN

RATP **SNCF** APTR ADATRIF

N° à reporter sur le coupon

G 955873

JARDIN DES PLANTES

1:5000

Mètres

Entrées de la Ménagerie

Halle aux Vins

Rue de Bourgogne

Porte

Rue Linné

Fontaine Cuvier

Porte

Rue Cuvier

Porte

Crocodiles   Reptiles

Labord toire   Hivernage   Volière

Nouv.Volière
Oiseaux
de proie

Animaux paisibles

Quai St Bernard

Port St Berna

Chevreuil

Amphithéâtre

Oiseaux
Chanteurs

Faisanderie

Oiseaux

Volière

w.c.

Animaux paisibles

w.c.

Tigres

Administration

Orangerie

Porte
Animaux
paisibles

Grands
Animaux

Singes

Sangliers

Hyènes

Renards
Loups

Labyrinthe
Belvédère

Cèdre

Daubenton

Animaux féroces

Animaux paisibles

Serres chaudes

Serres tempérées

Ours

Allée de Marronniers

École

Animaux féroces

Plantes
aquat.

Place Valhube

Entrée

Allée

de Botanique

École
de Botanique

Galeries

Plantes vi

de

logie

Tilleuls

Fleurs

Plantes
médicinales

Plantes alimentes
et
industrielles

Porte
principale

Tilleuls

des Arbres
Pépins

Pavillon
G. Ville

Galerie d'Anatomie

Salle
de dessin

w.c.

Boulev
de l'Hôpital

Porte

Gare
Orléa

upron

Wagner & Debes Le

au pair

MY FIRST REAL JOB IN PARIS came with a room. I lived in the maid's quarters of an eighteenth-century house in the seventh *arrondissement* with the American family for whom I worked as an au pair. Au pair was a fancy term, which, I discovered, meant baby-sitter, lunch maker, dog walker, confidante, and sweeper of the grand staircase. I had placed ads on bulletin boards at the American Church, the British Council, and the American Embassy.

> *American Girl Seeks Employment as Au Pair,*
> *Typist, Private Secretary, House Painter,*
> *Companion. Experienced. Reasonable rates.*
> **45-66-77-40**

I had written "American girl" only because all the other ads said it, and "woman" in that context seemed too, well, womanly.

The husband of the family chose me. He was a professor of philosophy at the Sorbonne. The wife edited an English-language gourmet cooking magazine based in Paris. Their seven-year-old twin daughters, Sudan and Chad, were mirror images of their parents. Sudan, the father's favored child, was kind, quiet, and sensitive. Chad, the mother's child, was cool, aloof, and sophisticated beyond her years. The husband was a farm boy from Idaho and treated me like the little sister of a friend from college. The wife was from an old-money Virginia family and would have said she treated me well. Although *Gone With the Wind* was her favorite movie, she lavished me with attention as if trying to make up for her ancestors' treachery. She appreciated my role as second wife to her husband and mother to her two children. I was born in America, but you could look at me and see a map of Africa. In the beginning, I looked at her—thin, blonde, rich, the opposite of me—but hard as I tried I couldn't see nothing but Miss Ann.

how to be an au pair

1. Look innocent, act naive.

Stand teary-eyed in front of the notice board at the British Embassy and wait for a man, a tall, kind-faced American stranger, to ask you if you are looking for work. Tell him yes. Tell him that you can do many things—help his children with their homework, clean his house, cook his meals, type his letters, and answer his telephones in six languages. Ask him if he knows James Baldwin, and if he answers correctly, let him look you over, let him give you his phone number and his wife's name. Call the wife. Meet her at a café near their home and impress her with your innocence and only a little of your intellect. Tell your prospective employers that you are a writer and that you are willing to work for food. Say anything to make them want you. Be humble. Let them know that you are willing to learn. Pretend that your purpose in life is to serve them well. In your first interview with the wife in the café sip your espresso slowly and let her talk about how much she misses her home in Virginia and the little luxuries she has to do without because everything is so expensive in Paris. Comfort her when she uses you to purge herself of her sins, one by one, confessing that she has been so busy she has not made love to her husband since the last au pair decided to return to Wales, weeks ago, but has been eyeing the muscular young Frenchman who delivers the mail to her office on a motorcycle, and that although she loves her children she has neglected them too. Let her confess her envy of French women and her lust for rare white truffles. Absolve her of all her sins. Tell her how much you enjoy cooking and cleaning and caring for children. Let her know that you can keep secrets.

You will grow to care for the American family, but remember that you are paid to wipe their tears, prepare their meals, and listen to their complaints, paid to celebrate their triumphs. Remember that this job will last for only a few weeks, until the family returns to the States. Soon you will leave this house and become a ghost of memory.

The children are attracted to you like a magnet, within moments of being introduced they begin playing with you like a new toy. You are aware that the mother is watching you to observe how sensitive and sensible you are. You swing the girls in turn by their arms in a circle, their dresses catching in the wind. The mother's daughter screams, "More, more," as the father's daughter screams, "Mommy, can we keep her?" You move into their home and become like one of the family.

2. Try not to lose the children.

The first day I am left alone with Sudan, the father's child, I take her to the park. Chad and the father have gone to pick out a new musical instrument for her to play at school, and the mother is working in her study on an article for her magazine. The former au pair, a pretty, busty Welsh girl named Kendall, who left the family to return to school in Wales, comes to visit before her departure from France. She tells us of her adventures—Jet-Skiing in Cannes, backpacking in the Pyrénées, and hitchhiking through Provence. Her dark hair is pulled up on top of her head in a ponytail. She smiles a lot and uses her hands when she talks. She is a tall girl and wears a tight blue fuzzy sweater covered with little furry blue balls and black ski pants. She takes off her hiking boots and sits on the sofa in the living room with her bare feet propped up on the coffee table. The mother looks at the ex–au pair's feet in surprise, but she says nothing. It is clear that Kendall has no respect for the wife or her antique furniture. I watch as Sudan sits on Kendall's lap and rests her head in her deep cleavage, rolling her face across the front of the ex–au pair's sweater as if she is in a trance.

Kendall laughs and keeps talking to me and the wife as if Sudan is invisible and still. When she tires of this game, Sudan interrupts the conversation and says that she wants to ride her bike in the gated park down the street. The mother looks tired and seems pleased by the suggestion. I am as excited as Sudan to escape the dull apartment on such a beautiful day. The ex–au pair offers to join Sudan and me, and we three walk the two blocks to the park. We sit watching Sudan as she pedals faster and faster in circles that get farther and farther away from us. We sit against the fence smoking cigarettes. Kendall talks about the different au pair positions she's had and the horrors experienced by her friends.

"Americans are okay. This family is very nice, but I wouldn't work for the French again. They expect too much. I was told to wash the grandmother's sheets and had only one afternoon per week free. I wanted to see the city, meet friends in the evening, but I was worked . . . excuse me . . . like a slave." She talks like a free woman with a family to catch her if she falls.

"Because they offer you room and board they act as if they're doing you a favor to let you sleep in a tiny little maid's room. The Americans, though, try to treat you like one of the family."

"It's going to be a little hard for me to pretend to be a distant cousin. How did you get any time for yourself?" I blow smoke into the air.

"You quit. If you want rest, go to the south of France and hook an old guy on the beach. Otherwise make friends and stay out of the house every chance you get, because you'll get worked to death."

I take my eyes off the child for only a minute or two, longer each time as Kendall's stories get more involved. Soon I am laughing so hard I am crying at her stories of revenge taken on the families she left because they were so difficult. She washed the French grandmother's Egyptian cotton sheets in hot water with bleach and a box of the children's crayons. She scrubbed a dirty toilet with the French father's toothbrush. I wish she were staying so that we could become friends. I tell her about growing up in the South, about my job in the museum, and how I came to Paris to be a writer.

"A writer! You're a brave girl," she says, impressed. "I wish you all the luck in the world." I believe she means it.

When I look up Sudan is not in sight. Kendall and I search the small park from one end to the other—the basketball court, the swings, the sand box and both entrances. We call out to her in English, French, and Welsh, but the child has disappeared. My heart races. I wonder if she has been hit by a car or kidnapped by a pervert. Just as I am about to accept the fact that Sudan is lost and begin to wonder how I will tell the parents, I see Sudan and the mother coming toward us. Sudan is happily riding her bike next to her mother, whose face is held in a controlled but fevered expression of rage. I am so happy I kiss the little girl and apologize to her mother and hope that she will forgive me someday for almost losing her child.

Kendall kisses each of us before she escapes into the city without me.

3. Rise early and turn up late.

At six A.M. the girls are still sleepy and have to be bribed to tumble from their warm beds into their bathroom to wash, put on their miniature dresses. They sit propped up at the elegant mahogany table and must be practically spoon-fed hot cereal or toast and bowls of fruit.

"I'll buy you a croissant later." I rush the food into their mouths.

"I want a *mille feuille,*" Sudan says.

"Then that is what you shall have," I say, stroking her head.

"I want an éclair," Chad says.

"After school you can choose anything you want. We can't be late again." Chad leans into me and seems to purr against my waist.

"Eden, do you look like your mother?" Chad stares up at me with her large, luminous green eyes.

"No. My mother looks like herself." I stroke her silky hair.

"When I grow up I want to look like you."

"But I'm not your mother," I say gently, rushing the girls down the stairs.

"I wish you were." Chad wraps her thin pale arms around me as far as they will go. She doesn't know yet just how much easier her life will be because she doesn't look like me.

4. Don't kill the dog.

Every evening I walk the monster, Faulkner, a ten-year-old gray wolfhound, blind in one eye and nearly crippled with arthritis. After I've loaded the dishwasher, put the food away, taken out the trash, and helped the children with their homework, I attach the leash to Faulkner's leather collar and practically carry him down the curving black-carpeted staircase I vacuum daily, although the bits of lint, dog hairs, and dirt reappear within hours. Faulkner and I shuffle out the glass-paned double doors, past the first-floor apartment of the landlady, a Belgian widow I've never seen and who I'm told is bedridden. She has a live-in nurse and is visited once a week by her children, who live on an estate near Versailles.

I unlock the tall black wrought-iron gate and walk down the narrow path lined with wildflowers and tall yellow grass and through the archway past the heavy door that opens onto avenue des Sablons, and I stroll along the wide sidewalk patiently as Faulkner tries to keep up with me. I walk slowly, keeping my eyes on the sidewalk, avoiding other pedestrians and the steaming piles of dog shit that menacingly litter the city's streets. Sometimes I stop to look at colorful posters taped up in shop windows announcing gallery openings. The most beautiful posters, printed on thick, high-quality glossy paper, publicize art events. Brightly colored abstracts, watercolors, film stills, cartoons, and Impressionist paintings. I sometimes ask shopkeepers and bartenders if I can take the posters when the date of the event has passed so that I can put them up on the walls in my little maid's room in the American family's house to make it a more homey place. I don't expect to stay long, but when I wake up in the night I want pleasant images to comfort me. On a park bench I see a couple wrapped around each other like circus contortionists. I cannot tell where she begins and he ends. It looks like love, but nothing in Paris is what it seems.

On these walks with Faulkner I think about poems and sometimes write pieces of them, catch stray sentences in a notebook that fits in the pocket of my coat. I keep a diary so that I will remember the things I have seen in Paris, record these new feelings too. I can feel myself changing in little ways. I dream in French; I crave croissants, red wine, and words that will illuminate.

I pass the butcher shop, and Faulkner growls at the bloody rabbits, plucked chickens, skinned ducks, and smoked hams hanging in the windows. When I pass the funeral home whose façade is lacquered a deep burgundy with letters in flowing white script, the owner, a thick, middle-aged man dressed in tweeds like a college professor, is usually leaning in the doorway smoking a pipe, blowing smoke rings in the air. In the small crowded room behind him is a massive mahogany desk covered with papers, a calculator with tape overflowing onto the desk. Funerals in France must be expensive. The funeral director speaks to me in a sweet, sly voice, and his eyes follow my breasts. His *"Bonsoir, mademoiselle"* invites conversation, but I avert my eyes and give him a quick *"Bonsoir, monsieur"* and pull the dog along past the wine shop, the Arab grocer, the vintage bridal shop, the toy store, and doorways that lead to single rooms and apartments above the businesses.

The French are as crazy for films as they are for dogs. Movies are costly and sell out quickly. After half an hour, Faulkner and I have circled the long block past the cinema where American movies dubbed in French are showing. Spike Lee's *She's Gotta Have It* is playing, but I can't get in. I can't even afford to go to the cheap movies out in the suburbs, so I am content to look at the provocative posters and walk on past shoe stores, a cafeteria, and a gray stone church built in the seventeenth century. On the corner at the end of

the street is the *tabac,* a combination bar and café that sells cigarettes, gum, phone cards, and stamps at the counter, and coffee, sandwiches, beer, and wine at the bar. At the tabac I buy
a pack of gum and give a *"Merci, madame"* to the woman behind the counter, who looks like a model in a magazine. Her
hair is pulled up into a French twist and her makeup is a perfect mask of blended flesh tones, her pale pink sweater set
looks brand-new. She seems amused by my French and
wishes me good night, almost singing as she counts the francs
into her register. I must watch the dog lagging behind; should
he be run over by a speeding Peugeot, the children would
never forgive me.

The French are dog crazy. All French dogs are high-strung
and sensitive, according to their owners. It is not uncommon to
see genuine alligator dog carriers in the Metro and fully clothed
dogs sitting at restaurant tables next to their owners, eating
from their very own plates. I asked Delphine why the city allowed owners to let their dogs shit on the sidewalks indiscrim-
inately.

"Why won't the dog owners pick it up? In the States you
would get a fine for letting your dog do its business in the middle of the sidewalk."

"Here we have people to do that," Delphine said.

"Not regularly enough," I said, annoyed.

And I knew she meant the North Africans brought into
Paris in the Fifties to do jobs the French refuse to do. Where I
come from, dogs are not pets to be played with or spoiled like
children, they are kept in the yard to bark at strangers. For this

service, they are given scraps from the table twice a day and a
bowl of water kept full.

5. Be willing to learn.

On Tuesdays the wife and I go to the market. She shows me
how to pick the freshest fruits, vegetables, and flowers, and
how to bargain for fish to get the best prices. Her French is
perfect, although her accent sounds as flat as a Tennessee tobacco field. In her tiny but well-stocked kitchen she teaches me
how to make fluffy garlic mashed potatoes with *crème fraîche,*
how to sauté crispy snow peas and prepare glazed roast pork.
She writes and edits articles on how to serve a dinner to impress
a gourmand guest, what to serve an international guest, what to
serve a guest you want to seduce. She instructs me in the fine art
of serving her family, which wines to serve with fish or chicken
or dessert. She has memorized the names and characteristics of
more than three hundred varieties of French cheese; I memorize the different kinds of lettuce and wild mushrooms, the
husband's favorite sauce, and learn how to disguise her children's most dreaded vegetables.

In school every French child learns how to tell a poisonous
mushroom from one that can be cooked in a soup. My lessons
on *champignons* are delivered in the French-American kitchen
on avenue des Sablons. I wash and chop and listen carefully so
that when the wife travels on business or works late cooking in
other kitchens I can take care of her family. She shows me how
to make a French-style apple pie, and when it is my turn I make
it perfectly. She is a good teacher, and I am the perfect student.

pommes tarte tartin

6–7 small tart apples, peeled and quartered
⅓ stick butter
½ cup sugar
Teaspoon lemon juice
Prepared pastry dough

Peel and quarter 6–7 small apples. Melt butter in a deep metal pie pan or cast-iron skillet. Stir in sugar. Layer apples in pan. Drizzle lemon juice over apples. Cook over low flame until syrup browns. Roll out chilled prepared pastry dough. Place dough over top of apples and prick with holes. Bake at 375 degrees (20–30 minutes) until crust browns. Turn out apple side up onto a serving dish. Serve hot with *crème fraîche*.

At the end of the day the wife sends me to the supermarket to buy milk, cheese, and Nutella and crispy baguettes from the bakery. With my own money I buy a can of lychees in syrup from the Chinese store on the corner to bribe Sudan to eat her dreaded peas. She wants to grow up to be thin and blonde and rich like her mother. I want to have the kind of life where I can eat like her mother and never gain a pound.

gratin dauphinois

2 pounds potatoes
2 large cloves garlic

2 tablespoons butter
1½ cups finely grated Swiss cheese
Salt/pepper/grated nutmeg to taste
1½ cups heavy cream

Heat oven to 400 degrees. Peel potatoes and slice as thin as coins. Slice garlic into paper-thin disks. Grease a shallow baking dish with butter. Layer baking dish with potatoes, sprinkling each layer with garlic, cheese, salt, pepper, and nutmeg, finishing with a layer of cheese. Dot with butter. Pour cream over potatoes, barely covering. Bake at 350 degrees 1–2 hours or until potatoes are tender and golden.

Entertain your hungry guests with card tricks or stories about the worst meal you've ever eaten. Serve with good humor and a chilled bottle of Chardonnay.

5. **Set an example for the children. Educate them.**

"Sudan, please eat your peas. I'll tickle your feet if you do."
She shakes her head at each temptation and refuses to open her pouty lips.

"Can you do this?" I swallow a mouthful of air and expel a surprisingly loud belch across the lunch table. Both she and Chad giggle. Now I have their complete attention.

"Do it again," they both shout.

I take a forkful of bright green peas and a tiny scoop of garlic mashed potatoes into my mouth, chew slowly and swallow discreetly.

"Only if you eat your peas."

They each eat three peas and I burp three magnificent rounds of garlicky breath into the air. We all laugh hysterically. *Again. Again. Again.* They shout so loud that Faulkner begins to bark and limp around the dining room table, hopping on his two good legs to make us quiet down. I teach them how to count in Spanish . . . *uno* . . . *dos* . . . *tres* . . . *cuatro* . . . *cinco* . . . and they eat their sautéed English peas, steamed broccoli, creamed spinach, braised brussels sprouts, and asparagus in lemon butter. I burp out arias of sound, conduct symphonies from the air in my belly. Their applause and clean plates are my rewards.

At night I read to them from *The Fire Next Time,* Baldwin's essay. They do not understand every word, but they know I'm serious and they listen carefully as I teach revolution. When we play dress-up I'm always Josephine Baker or Sojourner Truth. I use every opportunity to teach the future ruling class. When their parents go out at night I become the Invisible Man. I turn out all the lights in the house and show them real terror and forgiveness. I sing to the children, blues songs and spirituals they hum on their way to school.

They will know Marian Anderson and Bessie Griffin and the Gospel Pearls.

Go down, Moses . . .

Ma Rainey, Muddy Waters, and Koko Taylor

"Gimme a Pigfoot and a Bottle of Beer"

Billie Holiday

"Strange Fruit"

They will know about slavery and the true history of their names. Chad to the west, colonized by the French. Sudan to the east, colonized by the British. African countries in the center of the continent with false borders that touch. Ancient empires once prospered and now crumble under the weight of wars and modern slavery. It is my voice that soothes them back to sleep when they wake up with nightmares, my name they call when they are afraid. I feel the power but try not to abuse it.

On Mondays I take the girls to ballet, on Wednesdays they have tennis, on Fridays piano lessons, and Saturday mornings to the park so the husband and the wife can have sex.

Seeing us off at the door she rolls her eyes up toward her bedroom.

"You have your duties and I have mine," she says as if sex is another item to check off a very long and unsavory list.

I watch the girls study and play and dance, and grow to like them more and resent them less. It will be hard to say good-bye.

6. Show that you have other interests.

On Sunday, my day off, I go to the Luxembourg Gardens and walk through the delicate black wrought-iron gates and down a wide sandy path lined with soldierly trees and stroll along behind stylishly dressed French mothers in high heels and silk stockings pushing huge baby strollers. They grasp at delicate scarves wrapped elegantly around their necks and smoke slim cigarettes while their children watch the sky.

I sit on a bench in the chill and watch children sail toy boats in the fountain and try to imagine my life as a writer. I asked the husband once if he knew Baldwin or Richard Wright. He knows Wright only through books. He thinks that *Native Son* is the best novel written by a black American in the twentieth century. Faulkner, though, is his personal god. He met Baldwin once at a party given by a journalist friend at bar in the Marais.

"He looked like a gnome. I thought he would be taller. He drank a lot and cursed the host before he left with half the people to take the party somewhere else. *The Fire Next Time* changed me. Changed the way I looked at black men, at white men, at women, at my children, at my own face in the mirror. I couldn't pretend I didn't know anymore how angry, and rightly so, many black people were. How unjust the world is. I had led a sheltered life. Baldwin speaks the truth, and beautifully; his essays should be national anthems. Do you know why I named my children Sudan and Chad? Because I worked in each country before independence and I found them equally beautiful, exotic and mysterious, just like my newborn babies." He fails to see the irony in his paternalism and I see no reason to bring it up, especially after he makes me such a generous offer.

The husband is starting a writing group. To make up for not knowing much about Baldwin he invites me to join. The writing group consists of wives of diplomats and businessmen, widows, and other ladies of leisure, almost all over thirty-five. He asks me if I would like to join, and before he can take it back I say yes and wonder what a group of writers do together. Writing is such a solitary action. I will write books about what I see when no one thinks I'm looking or listening. I hope that after reading my books no one will ever enter a room the same way, that they will look at the world differently, say please and thank you to staff whose spit makes tasty revenge.

A week later I am the last one to arrive at the grand apartment where the writing group is to meet. All the while I am thinking that I have to leave before the hour is over to pick up the children and how inconvenient it is to have to be responsible for anything else today. The seven women present all are white and fashionably dressed. I imagine their stories will be just as vapid and light as the tones in which they speak. Our hostess is a tight-faced South African lady in a Chanel-style suit with big gold buttons. She serves us tea and dry English biscuits on fancy yellow china and begins a discussion on the pros and cons of of South African divestment. She warns us of the harm it will cause the average South African and how much harder it will be for the poor blacks. Before I can begin to get angry and uncomfortable at the inevitable question that will be directed at me, the only black person in the room with authority to speak for the millions of disenfranchised black South Africans, there is a knock at the door. Our hostess puts down the silver tea tray and crosses the room to the door, tottering on her square-toed pumps.

"It's the plumber," she says sweetly over her shoulder. She speaks with him for a few minutes, then turns back to the room again.

"Does anyone have any money? I need to tip the plumber." I sit in silence and bring the lukewarm cup of tea to my lips. I wonder if she really expects me to give her money. I have forty francs in my pocket and won't get paid by the husband for another two weeks. I can only hope for a bonus when they leave Paris. I marvel at our hostess's boldness. The husband reaches for his wallet. She thanks him ever so much and I'm sure he will never see those fifty francs again. The husband begins discussing a new French novel and tells us it is a good example of style over substance. Before my eyes he is transformed from the middle-aged overworked husband and father into a knowledgeable college professor whose students flirt with him. All that information makes him sexy. Suddenly I realize that it is three o'clock and I have to pick up his children. I stand abruptly, brushing biscuit crumbs from my jeans.

"It was nice to meet you all. I hope to see you again," I say, but I don't really mean it. I don't belong here, and I'm sure I'll never see any of them again. When I write, it will be alone in a room, and substance will triumph over style. I take the stairs three at a time and hope the bus comes quickly.

The leaves are turning brown, and the air is cool. The sky is gray and threatening rain. I walk down the steep hill toward the stop for the bus that will get me to the children's school in ten minutes. I turn the corner onto a street that leads down to place de l'Odéon, a large square in front of the Odéon Théâtre, where, Indego told me, Adrienne Kennedy's *Funnyhouse of a Negro* was performed in 1967. I miss him now that he has gone to Germany. He had prepared me well for Paris. I am surprised to see so many people in the square at the bottom of the hill and still more pouring in from rue Corneille from the direction of the Luxembourg Gardens. It is so quiet. Too quiet for so many people in such a small place. The noise of hundreds of feet on the cobblestone streets, feet beating down the battlefield, but no one speaks.

A girl with her hair tied back with a black velvet ribbon is holding hands with a brown-skinned young man who looks like a boy I went to college with. I almost call out to him, but I remember that he may not speak my language. The young man is dressed in jeans and a black distressed leather motorcycle jacket. He and the girl are walking down the hill. The sky is blue and filled with flat clouds and is wide like an ocean upside down. The white-trunked plane trees around the square are neatly trimmed. Dozens of soldiers empty out of large navy blue buses with bars on the windows, young men, silent and grim, holding rifles and machine guns slung across their bulletproof vests. Their eyes are like those of scared children, darting around at the crowd that is forming. Their bodies are tense and rigid and march in straight lines toward the square just outside the line of plane trees. I am nervous. The busy shops that usually bustle with tourists and whose wares spill over onto the sidewalk are shuttered and locked up tight. A few tentative faces peer from the shops. My feet move uncertainly, as if I am walking onto a minefield. Young people in blue jeans and school uniforms, blue-collar workers in jumpers, and office workers all gather side by side in the square. No one sits on the benches. I can see them from where I am standing at the top of the hill, and I am trying to decide whether or not to walk past the line of policemen and join the strike when someone starts to sing. A girl in a flowered shirt and jeans gives me a flyer. It is in French and I make out only a few words, but Delphine has told me about the student demonstrations. She said the new law would allow universities to raise fees, make their admissions more selective, and issue their own diplomas, making some diplomas more prestigious than others. The French students were not having it. It was estimated that nearly a million students would protest all over France. The students seem already to be victorious and their spirit is infectious. My feet make up my mind for me, and before I know what is happening, I am walking and singing and the guns are pointed at me too. I try not to think about Sudan and Chad waiting for me in front of their school as all the other children are taken away. It is a hard choice to make. I have grown to like the girls and their parents, who are relatively liberal and have the best intentions. After a while my conscience turns and I run in the opposite direction, toward the métro, where I discover students crowding the platform, standing in the doorways of the cars to keep the trains from moving. I have to walk all the way to Montparnasse, past throngs of people in the same predicament. Rush-hour traffic has come to a halt on the boulevard.

By the time I get within a block of the school it is four o'clock, an hour past the time I was to pick up the children. I am sweating, nervous that the girls may have tried to walk home and have gotten lost, never to be found again. I start to run, but the street in front of their school is empty. Not a single child or teacher is in sight, and the building is locked. No one answers the bell. I run the five blocks to the apartment, and when I enter, the mother seems surprised to see me standing in the doorway of the living room, out of breath.

"Where are the children?" she asks, looking up at me over her glasses. She drops the *Paris Match* she was reading.

"I don't know. When I got to the school it was closed. The girls weren't there. There's a demonstration. I had to walk from Montparnasse."

She looks as if she is about to raise her hand to hit me. I feel as if I deserve to die for losing her children a second time. As she begins moving toward me the phone rings. I pick up the receiver before she can kill me. It is a woman with a thick Haitian accent. She lives half a block down the street. She has taken the girls to her apartment. She found them wandering a few blocks from the school. They remembered their phone number. I run out the door before the mother can speak and go to rescue them. When the old woman opens the door to her first-floor apartment, I smell garlic and fried fish. She wipes her hands on her apron, and the girls come rushing out. Sudan wraps her arms around me.

"We thought you had forgotten us."

Chad stands a little distance from us, looking hurt, but I pull her to me and kiss them both on the tops of their little blonde heads and promise that I would never forget them. I explain to them that the students are marching in the streets, then stop myself from trying to justify my error in judgment. I beg them to forgive me for being late, and after thanking the old woman I swing them by their thin pale arms into the cool Paris evening. I swing them around in circles as they scream and shout, and I feel lucky that I have found them and that they are safe. I understand that I have failed the wife again, but the husband's guilt gives me yet another chance. He takes responsibility for making me late. If there is a fire next time, he wants me on his side. After the children are put to bed the husband and wife remind me that they will be leaving Paris in a few weeks' time and that they will no longer need me. I don't know what I'll do. Delphine's parents have asked her to spend the fall school session on the family farm because they are afraid of all the terrorist activity. She'll be leaving soon too, and her apartment is being sublet.

That night I listen to a BBC radio news report. I had for a few moments been part of the biggest demonstration by students that France had ever seen. The display of strength and the solidarity with labor unions forced the government to withdraw the offensive legislation. The BBC newscaster says that the protest I walked along the edges of recalls 1968, when the students wanted to change society by changing the university system. Nearly twenty years later, it is 1986, it's happening again. Policemen beat to death a twenty-year-old student, Malik Oussekine, at the end of peaceful student demonstrations. I pray for the safety of my artist friend Malik and the soul of the student who was murdered. To make the students seem dangerous and to justify their use of excessive force, the police had stood by, looking on, encouraging thugs to loot stores and burn cars. The students lost the battle, but won the war. The offensive legislation was withdrawn. The next day, an eerily quiet morning, the Latin Quarter looks like a combat zone. On my last day with Delphine she says she saw the burning cars from her window the night before. She was scared but excited, knowing what was happening on the streets. Her parents insisted on driving into Paris to pick her up. They are arriving in a few hours. When we kiss I am afraid it is the last time I will see her. I thank her and we promise to keep in touch.

Outside, the smell of burning rubber still fills the air. I pick up a piece of broken glass and put it in my pocket. I want something by which to remember being in a war zone.

❧

One Saturday morning, I am told to take the children to a birthday party at the home of the Fabres. Their daughter takes tennis lessons with the twins. The Fabre child is a pretty girl whose manners and haughtiness mirror her mother's. I had noticed that like her mother she wore diamond stud earrings and a tiny diamond tennis bracelet on her delicate wrist. I have met Madame Fabre at the park. She is tall and slim with thick chestnut hair, and she shines like a well-groomed horse. Every time I see her, she is wearing lots of gold-and-diamond jewelry and an elegant little black dress. When I call for directions, she says that the apartment is in the sixteenth, as if giving me a happy secret.

The sixteenth *arrondissement* begins at the end of the Champs-Elysées at the mouth of the Arc de Triomphe and stretches for two miles and is lined with luxury shops, movie theaters, car dealerships, and restaurants. According to *Paris Passion,* a hip English-language magazine, the area is home to a mix of wealthy French aristocrats, Arab sheiks, and *nouveau riche* Americans. In the sixteenth *arrondissement* the grass seems greener, the air fresher, it is definitely cleaner than other areas of the city with the exception of the eternal piles of dog shit at irregular intervals on the sidewalk. Stately rows of elegant houses and apartment buildings sit behind electronically controlled gates. Vivid green grass carpets a park that runs the length of the street.

Pairs of armed security guards patrol the embassies of foreign countries and the private residences of local and international politicians. Mercedes sedans, Alfa Romeos, and Jaguars are parked under trees with low-hanging branches. I walk along slowly holding the girls' hands, drinking in the ornate French architecture. So many beautiful things to look at—carvings of graceful swans, faces of angels, detailed rosettes, immaculate miniature gardens exploding with color and variety. I contemplate how I could discreetly ask Madame Fabre if she is still looking for a nanny. A Swedish au pair I met at the twins' tennis class told me Madame Fabre had offered her eight thousand francs to work as a full-time nanny, but she couldn't take the job because she was going home soon. It was a lot more than I was being paid, and I would need a place to live when the Americans left. With eight thousand francs I could save enough to rent a small room for a few months in the south of France and begin to write.

On the phone I had stumbled through my limited French to get the address.

"You are American?" Madame Fabre had asked.

"Yes, madame."

"I expect the girls to arrive at noon."

The loud click in my ear signaled the abrupt end of our conversation. I sat still for a moment before picking up a pen and pad and calculating what I could do with eight thousand francs. First thing, I would buy myself a pair of shoes from one of the shops near place de l'Odéon. High-gloss Italian leather pumps, sleek Japanese creations that looked like miniature cars, stiff English riding boots. I would be practical but not too, something very simple, very French. Then I would not be afraid to

enter Les Deux Magots, where Wright sometimes met Baldwin
for drinks and conversation. The right shoes would give me a
certain confidence. Eight thousand francs could buy a train
ticket to Versailles, where I could see how kings and queens had
lived in opulence, eating cake. The Swedish au pair had men-
tioned that the job would require extensive travel. I imagined
that a woman like Madame Fabre would go to places like Bali,
Tahiti, and the Costa Brava to keep up her tan. I would learn
to swim and lie on beaches watching the sun go down and be
swept away . . . By the time I fell asleep in my hard, narrow little bed I was exhausted by preparations for my new life.

The vast Paris sky is layered with thick gray clouds that will
soon rain gently on millions of hats, coats, outstretched um-
brellas, and upturned collars. Somber rain clothes darken the
afternoon shadows. The girls are dressed in matching blue velvet and lace party dresses. They each carry a small gold box
with a crystal egg inside to add to the birthday girl's collection.
I have tied white velvet ribbons in their hair. It is surprising to
me that children's birthday parties here are elegant, usually
catered affairs. When we arrive at the beautiful black iron gate
with floral shapes that Madame Fabre had described I press a
mother-of-pearl buzzer. I hear a click and the gates open for us
to enter the cobblestone courtyard around which three other
apartment buildings rise. Colorful flower boxes decorate most
of the large bay windows.

I knock at the glass door with the brass concierge sign above
it. After a few minutes a woman's face appears. The concierge
looks like hell. Her hair, wrapped around large pink curlers, is
half covered by a black satin scarf. Wisps of tinted hair escape

and lie limp on her forehead. A pale, heavily made-up face with penciled-in brows looks over my threadbare wool coat and dusty shoes with suspicion. When she sees the girls behind me her face relaxes.

"Qu'est-ce que vous voulez?" she shouts through the door, her breath fogging the glass momentarily. I can hear a small dog barking and a loud TV program from behind the door.

"Je cherche la maison de Madame Fabre."

"Deuxième étage, sur la gauche," she snaps and disappears behind the door. Probably to rejoin her French soap opera and feed melted bonbons to her high-strung dog.

We pass through the marble lobby with its crystal chandelier and plush burgundy carpeted staircase curving upward to the first landing. I am impressed by the stained glass window on the next landing, a royal crest of some kind, with lions and crossed swords beneath an elaborate crown. The colors are rich and jewel-like. I push back the black accordion gate to the tiny old-fashioned lift, open the glass door, and we step into the carpeted, oak-paneled interior. A single yellow rose blooms in a slim tube vase attached near the shiny brass operating panel. The girls sit down on a brown velvet Queen Anne loveseat bolted to the floor as if they are in a box at the opera and the drama is about to begin. It is the most luxurious elevator I have ever seen. It is so beautiful I could live in it, sleep standing up. Even the air is gently perfumed with the scent of roses. On either side of me the girls hum the same cartoon theme song. We get off on the second floor and approach the apartment on the left. I knock politely and wait. Nothing. I knock harder. The girls sit down on the staircase and wait patiently. Still nothing.

We are late and I want Madame Fabre's first impression of me to be a good one since I intend to get her to interview me for the nanny job. For ten minutes I search for a doorbell. In desperation I use the elaborate brass door knocker again, banging with all my might. Still no response. Not even an echo. After standing outside the door for another few minutes, I finally pull on the fancy door knocker, and magically a chime sounds in the distance, then soft muffled footsteps. One of the massive wooden doors opens, and a very pretty, petite dark-skinned woman with a shy smile wearing a short French maid's uniform that looks too small for her stands in the opening. A tiny white cap is perched on her thick wavy hair that is caught up in a ponytail. She wears sheer black stockings and oversized men's slippers on her feet. The maid keeps her head tilted downward and peeks at me sideways.

"Je suis bien chez Madame Fabre?"

The maid replies in rapid Spanish, which I can't understand, and gestures for us to follow her. I wish I'd studied harder in Spanish class and had kept more than numbers and the days of the week in my memory. We follow the maid. I keep my eyes on the treasures unfolding around me. The foyer walls are lined with dark burgundy silk, a gold-framed mirror on our right, a flowing fountain gurgles ahead of us at the end of the hall.

As we pass a doorway on the left, I slow down to take a look into the formal living room. Twin sparkling chandeliers, gray suede walls, two silver sofas the length of stretch limos facing each other across a zebra-skin rug. Dozens of yellow roses in a square blue glass vase sit atop a glossy black grand piano. A life-size marble statue stands poised staring through the windows onto the unreal green of the avenue below. Several large oil paintings hang in each of the rooms. Farther down the hallway, the maid takes my worn coat and the girls' velvet jackets, smiles, and motions us toward the sound of accordion music and children laughing. The room where the party is being held is as elegant as the rest of the apartment. A long table is set up buffet-style with little sandwiches, bricks of cheese, a silver bowl of strawberries, and dishes of candy wrapped in silver and gold foil. In the center of the table what looks like a wedding cake is decorated with real roses and little bunches of sugared violets. Another table is piled high with elaborately wrapped presents. The girls add their presents to the pile and join the other children, who are watching a puppet show at the end of the room. The stage looks like the one set up in the Luxembourg Gardens. I don't understand what the puppets are saying, but one puppet is hitting the other and the children are laughing wildly.

There are no adults in the room. The other au pairs and parents probably dropped off the children for the two hours it will take to get through the festivities. Madame Fabre enters from behind us, and when she catches my eye motions for me to follow her out of the room. We walk back down the long hallway and enter a sitting room that feels like a deep maroon-colored womb. The walls are covered in silk upon which hang huge gilt-framed paintings. The sofas, chairs and Oriental carpet are all the same bloody color, the fireplace is black marble. A long, low glass table is spread with untouched copies of picture books about Hollywood, English gardens, and the art of Matisse. A wall of tiny diamond-shaped windowpanes looks down onto the quaint cobblestoned courtyard. Suddenly I feel shabbily dressed in these surroundings even though I am wearing my best clothes, a black cocktail dress from the Fifties I found in the flea market. I sit down too quickly, bumping my knee painfully against the glass table. Madame Fabre's long suntanned arm stretches a diamond-and-ruby-ringed hand toward me. I shake the limp, too soft hand and stare at the huge diamond on the fourth finger. I gape at the huge emerald-cut diamond-and-ruby necklace that lies heavy on her tanned chest. Madame is fortyish, tall as I am, but much slimmer. Her short hair is cut in a sharp, fashionable bob. She looks girlish despite the jewels and heavy makeup. Blue eyes, high cheeks, pinched nose and lips a thin frosted pink line. I glimpse her perfectly capped white teeth now and then throughout the interview. She wears a black dress with plunging neckline, black-seamed stockings, and black silk pumps. She looks ready for a cocktail party.

"I'm sorry, Madame Fabre. My French isn't very good yet. Do you mind if we speak English?"

"Not at all. Let me get to the point. I know that you are an au pair for the American twins. Are you happy with your situation?"

"Lisbeth told me you were looking for a nanny. I'm interested in hearing about the job."

Madame Fabre lights a cigarette and blows smoke above my head.

"You will be expected to speak English to the children, Caroline, whom you have met, and Pierre, my son. They are very intelligent. They are six and seven years old. We need someone to care for them, to prepare the breakfast at seven in the morning. And lunch as well. Of course the beds of the children must be made up and their rooms kept neatly. That will be your responsibility. You will accompany the children to the Ecole Internationale. It is the best school in Paris, you know. The children are studying languages. Caroline speaks Spanish, English, Italian, and a bit of German as well. Pierre is very special, he is inclined toward mathematics. We employ a driver, who will drive you and the children to school and also will be available to take you shopping for the children's meals. The driver will drive you and the children to activities. Caroline takes tennis, riding, and dance lessons. Pierre will study tennis and violin this season. They need to feel that someone is watching their progress. You will be required to attend all school functions. Monsieur Fabre travels for business quite a lot, and I entertain."

She draws on the cigarette and continues her graphic description of a full-time slave.

"Some ironing is involved. Monsieur is very particular. You would prepare dinner for the children. Monsieur Fabre and I dine out when he's in Paris. There is a bit of traveling involved. Christmas and New Year's we go to Switzerland. Do you ski? It doesn't matter. In February the children have a winter holiday. You will accompany the children to New York and Montreal to visit both sets of grandparents. Easter, we ski in the Italian Alps or sail near Sardinia. Each summer we take two months at our home in the south of France. The salary is five thousand francs per month."

"Excuse me, madame, but I was told the salary was eight thousand francs."

"You misunderstood. The salary includes a room here with us and meals. It is a very generous offer, I assure you. There are some aspects of the job that may strike you as unconventional, but first let me show you the rest of the apartment."

We pass through a huge modern kitchen and dining area. The maid is watching TV with her shoes off and holding on her lap a baby that looks like her own. The nanny's room is a closet off the kitchen. A high-ceilinged peach-colored room that was probably once a pantry. It contains a single bed with a high-backed wooden chair, a white chest of drawers, and a window that overlooks an alley filled with rubbish cans and wet wash on lines. I try not to show my disappointment. The children's rooms are large and airy and filled with brightly colored toys strewn across every inch of floor space.

"Follow me into the library." Her legs wobble a bit on the high heels.

The books in the library are mostly leather-bound or oversized books on gardening and art.

"We don't have much time to read. Our lives are so full." Madame Fabre waves her jeweled hand around like a wand.

She checks her diamond-studded watch and comments that it is almost time to cut the cake. I remember my mother's stories of being turned down for jobs or being refused housing or being offered lower wages than advertised when a potential employer discovered she was black. Often au pairs and nannies are imported sight unseen to work in foreign countries and abused or taken advantage of, worked like slaves. I have heard few positive stories. An Italian girl studying cultural anthropology at the Sorbonne was given her own apartment a few blocks from her employers, a fair salary, light baby-sitting for teenaged children, and the opportunity to go to school and work another job if she wanted. That was the best situation I knew of. Most girls are in their twenties, in vulnerable positions, and easy to take advantage of.

I am polite enough to allow Madame Fabre to finish the speech she has obviously delivered many times before.

"The last girl we had was like one of the family. Monsieur Fabre liked her very much. Two weekends a month I travel to Spain. Monsieur Fabre likes to spend more time with the children. Monsieur Fabre is usually very fond of the au pair." I thought of the pretty young woman in the kitchen and wondered about the baby on her lap. I was sad to have found that I wasn't so far from home after all. No thank you, Madame Fabre, I'd rather eat mud.

My plans to learn to ski in the Swiss Alps and sail to Sardinia dissolve into the rose-scented air as the elevator descends to the ground floor with the two little girls on either side of me singing along, *Go Down, Moses.*

The clouds burst as we run toward the Arc de Triomphe, pouring rain. The girls scream, and I am sorry too that their dresses are ruined but I don't have enough money for a taxi and we have to kill another half hour anyway for their parents to complete their weekly date for sex.

If I want to get to the south of France I will have to get another job, so a few days later, at the first working telephone that accepts my *télécarte,* I dial the number from a notice for part-time work I stuffed in my otherwise empty wallet two weeks before.

CIMETIÈRE MONTPARNASSE.

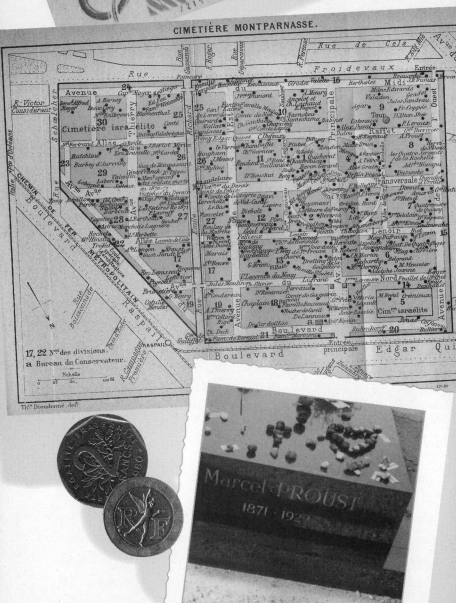

poet's helper

IN PARIS ALL WINDOWS have a view. Everyone who lives here believes in the poetry of freshly washed skies instead of ordinary rain. The clean, damp, early morning air is sweet with the scent of fresh-baked croissants and buttery madeleines. My mouth waters as I stand before a window of baked goods imagining myself licking the sugary panes of glass until my lips are ruined by powdered sugar and stained with the fruity blood of raspberries.

My reflection in the bakery window startles me. More than a hungry mouth, I am young, black, female, with an oval face the color of baked bread, brown eyes recording the newness of my first month in Paris, full lips asking for directions in broken French, and a proud nose registering the perfume in the air. My demeanor is pleasant. I have been taught to smile and be gracious in most circumstances. My hair, cut close to the scalp, is covered by a mustard-colored felt hat found in the métro. My body is womanly. I am wearing a long-sleeved, knee-length blue sundress, which is covered by my heavy coat from the flea market. I do not feel particularly American, but any Frenchman can tell because I am wearing white socks and black leather running shoes and carrying a black canvas backpack slung over my right shoulder like an ordinary tourist.

I am traveling east on a sidewalk in a quiet neighborhood swept clean before dawn by North Africans in fluorescent green jumpsuits who speak to each other in Arabic and African languages and who punctuate their musical conversations by spitting into the gutter. My destination is the apartment of the poet Elizabeth, where I work as her helper after I walk the twins to school and before I pick them up in the afternoon. The poet Elizabeth has so little imagination she thinks I steal from her. She thinks that I am trying to poison her, she thinks I hate her. In her imagination I am a heartless monster trying to devour her, an evil witch casting spells on her, an anxious beggar waiting for a taste of her bones.

Once I bought a golden square of creamy flan with change left over from a trip to the market, but she is stingy and doesn't want to pay me what I am worth. My people have a history of service to her people. Even here in Paris, thousands of miles from home and years after slavery has been officially abolished, I cannot escape her expectation that gratitude be married to servitude. Her skin is pale and privileged, mine is brown and sweaty from labor in her house. I am not thankful. Not even a little.

Once I put too much salt in the fish. An honest mistake. I do admit, the truth is this, sometimes I hate her so much that I think of little ways to hurt her, but I never do. I wait on her hand and foot, like a slave. She said to me once that in glory days I would have been presented to her as a gift, like a toy at Christmas or on her birthday, for her amusement, and she wouldn't have had to pay so dear a price. I want to slap her, but it is too easy to hurt her. There are many ways to torment a soul.

The notice on the bulletin board in the dimly lit foyer of the American Church reads: POET'S HELPER WANTED—PART-TIME. It is typewritten on a yellow unlined three-by-five index card and pinned to the board with a brass upholstery tack. I notice the tack because my American employer's wife likes to redecorate on her husband the professor's salary, and she is always using expensive little things to cover big, ugly cheap things she finds at the Porte de Clignancourt flea market or in piles by the side of the road. The phone number at the bottom of the card is handwritten, the letters are slightly smudged, faint, and the letter R is broken.

"*Bonjour.* Good morning, Elizabeth here." The poet's British accent is grand and elegant.

"I'm calling about the position of poet's helper," I say trying to erase all traces of my Southern accent.

"Yes," she says brightly. "Can you come round this morning?"

"I can come round anytime that's convenient for you," I say as politely as I know how. Southerners are known for having the most beautiful manners. My parents taught me that patience and good manners were tools for survival in the segregated South they grew up in, and I am learning that they are useful abroad as well.

The poet gives me directions to her apartment in the fifteenth *arrondissement.*

"The bus driver will let you off at the métro. Walk half a block east. My building faces the churchyard. Number one. Just ring. My girl will let you in," she says, and I hope that the girl she is referring to is her daughter. I don't want to be anybody's girl. My mother worked for white people all her life so I wouldn't have to, she constantly reminds me. I don't want to disappoint her, but I have not met James Baldwin, written a novel, or fallen in love. I want to stay a little longer in this place, and for that I am willing to do many things.

When I saw the notice I began plotting my escape from life as an au pair. I imagined that as a poet's helper I would accompany the poet to soirées in the Latin Quarter, sit beside the poet as we listened to conversations about philosophy, poetry, and existentialism. I imagined drinking red wine and laughing with the other poet's helpers, exchanging bits of gossip about the poets' love lives. I imagined traveling around Europe with the poet, taking care to tip porters for carrying our bags to rooms in quaint hotels overlooking oceans and gardens and village rooftops in Spain, Italy, Greece, and Russia, if the poet had

Marxist leanings. The poet I imagined would ask my opinion about what suit of clothes to wear, which poems to read, and what wine we should have with dinner. I would type correspondence, replying to invitations to parties and weddings, art openings, fashion shows, concerts, readings, book signings, and lectures. I would of course be paid well for my services and given ample time to visit museums, sun on the beach, and shop in the marketplaces of the world. And if the poet was as desirable as their words, sex would not be out of the question. Finally the poet would introduce me to my literary godfather, the inspiration for my journey so far from home to a country which promised to be both welcoming and illuminating. In my imagination the possibilities were endless.

Of all the things I've ever done, I'm least proud of my first reaction to the poet. Her sharp English profile against the colorful handwoven carpet on the wall scared me. I wanted to run from that small stuffy room. Her apartment was on the first floor of an ornate building next to a convent and faced a cemetery. I wanted to run out into the bright, wet streets, breathe fresh air. The smell of sickness had settled like dust on the room.

A French girl wearing a uniform of a simple gray dress with a plain white collar opened the door of the apartment onto the living room. The poet was sitting in a wheelchair facing me. A crooked smile twisted her comically painted lips. The young woman directed me to sit in a straight-backed chair next to the door, directly in front of the poet. The French girl sat in a similar chair next to the poet with her eyes resting on her hands folded in her lap.

"You look like a girl of sixteen, no more. Your skin is so

smooth, like an orchard apple dipped in carmel sauce," the poet
marveled, eating me with her bright eyes. Only her eyes were
desirable. "Your face is still so innocent . . ."

"I have some experience," I say, blushing. I felt as if she
could see through my artificial enthusiasm and I needed her to
like me, to choose me so that I could stay in Paris a little longer.

"You're American." Her eyes drift down to my shoes, then
float back to my face. For a moment her head seemed too heavy
for her long white neck, but she straightened it with a jerk. I felt
intense pity for her.

"Tell me about yourself. How did you come to be in Paris?"
she asked.

"I want to be a writer," I said boldly, because here in another country I am new, I could choose what and who I would
be. A writer. A person who survives a dangerous life and risks
all to tell about it. I sit on the edge of the hard wooden chair
with my knees pressed tightly together, bouncing my toes nervously.

"To be a good writer you must write often, seek out adventure, be original, and read good literature. Whom do you love?
Which writers?" Her chin dropped to her chest and she stared
at my uncovered knees, seemingly counting the stitches in the
hem of my skirt.

"Baldwin. He said Paris was a haven. I'm looking for that."

"I hope that Paris will be as kind to you."

The poet made me uncomfortable, the way her eyes cut a
thin, sharp line from my tightly laced shoes to a place on the
wall just above my head. I tried to shift the conversation.

"Do you still write poems?" I stared at her, pressing the flowered hem of my dress over my knees in case her eyes came back to that place.

"In my head," she said quietly, trying unsuccessfully to lift a cigarette to her lips. The French girl placed the cigarette between the poet's lips and then removed it and tapped the ash onto a small silver tray. She didn't speak at all during the interview and never once looked me in the eye. Elizabeth tried to be elegant, but her long twisted limbs did not cooperate, she had little control without concentration, and even then each movement was a struggle. She smiled with lips crooked with lipstick applied by an unsteady hand, her eyelids were slashed with strokes of shiny green shadow and her cheeks rouged with circles of pink. Her long silver hair was like a waterfall around her face. Her chipped red nails looked like bloody claws flailing in the air for a newly lit cigarette. Her skin was dry and finely wrinkled like delicate tissue paper that had been crumpled then smoothed by hand and stored in a drawer away from sunlight. But I could see what had been.

"I write poems in my head at night after I am tucked in by one of the Sisters of Mercy next door. I lie awake for hours listening to the radio. When young Sister Beatrice comes I recite my poetry to her, and she is shocked by all the foul words and perverse subjects, but she is polite. I think she secretly likes it. She's cloistered, so she is forbidden to speak, but her eyes tell a different story. And sometimes her hands. She means no harm. She smiles easily and blushes as if she were the one who commits all my terrible sins. And sometimes she whispers to me.

She knows that I am like a priest and I will never tell the Sisters, no one will ever know but she and I and God, whom I've forsaken as He has forsaken me."

The poet's high cackling laugh was transformed into a hacking cough that lasted for several minutes. The French girl watched the poet's body shake and convulse as though she was watching a very boring movie. When the poet's body was still, the girl held a cup of water to her dry, cracked lips and the poet drank, gulping and sucking as if her insides were on fire.

The poet Elizabeth told me that her disease did not have a cure. The doctors said she had a progressive disease of the central nervous system. Her body was limp.

"It's rather like being a poet, this malady. You live with it and eventually die from it. It is as mysterious as genius," she said, struggling to sit up in the chair. "More elusive than light at the end of the day."

"Do you know any famous writers?" I know it is an unoriginal question, but I ask it anyway.

She named a Czech writer, a Spanish poet, a Colombian novelist.

"Do you know Baldwin?" I asked.

"He is the most intelligent Negro I've ever met. I don't know how he manages to write so brilliantly. He's a marvelous cook, and so funny." She laughed.

I didn't know if she was teasing me or if she was a fool. I wished I could think of a question to ask her about him, but I was speechless. There would be plenty of time for me to find out if she knew anything that mattered. There was no way I would leave without the job. Perhaps the Czech, the Spaniard, the Colombian, or even Baldwin himself would drop in for tea one afternoon, and I would be waiting to learn their secrets and learn how to become what I wanted to be. She was not a famous poet and never would be, but she knew things that had value to me.

"I can do the job," I said, convinced I would have to make sacrifices to be a real writer.

"This is not merely a job. I need someone I can count on. It's hard for me on my own. I don't have much money, but I can offer you lunch and four hundred francs a week."

Four hundred francs was barely equal to minimum wages in the States, but that was not the most important issue.

"When would you like me to start?"

"Can I depend on you?" she asked. There were tears in her eyes, which the French girl wiped away with the corner of a paper napkin. I nodded yes, wiping away a tear of my own.

She hired me on the spot as her helper, but I would really be father confessor, mother comfort, sister, lover, and best friend. Mostly I would be the maid.

The irony of our situation is not lost on me. Sometimes I love the poet Elizabeth so much that I die a little each time at the sight of her lovely silver hair still thick and full of life, her large luminous green eyes shiny with the glint of medication. Her voice is a song when she tells me the stories of her life. My heart breaks each afternoon when the spell is broken and I drink the freshly washed air and bathe in the perfumed light, wiping from my skin the dust and her loneliness and her fear of death.

Sometimes the poet Elizabeth disgusts me. Her grand airs, her moods, her paranoia, her constant gas, and her taste for fried liver with lemon and onions. As I carefully count the francs she gives me at the end of the week, folded neatly in a small white envelope, I realize I am not a poet's helper for the money alone. I am a poet's helper because I have compassion, and because perhaps one day Baldwin will drop in for tea and I will ask him to part with just one secret.

how to be a poet's helper

1. I rise at six in the morning and make coffee for myself and breakfast for the children in the apartment where I live and work as an au pair. Holding their tiny hands in mine, I walk the sleepy twin girls to school five blocks from the apartment in Montparnasse then take a crowded bus to the métro stop Vaugirard. I walk half a block east and two blocks north, down a narrow street across the street from a church and a cemetery and next door to a convent of cloistered nuns. I arrive at seven-thirty in the morning and ring the bell, which sounds at the convent next door. Someone from the convent buzzes me inside the tall black wrought-iron gate. I rarely see the mysterious Sisters, who are silent except for daily prayers. I use my key to let myself into the first-floor flat and I call out a friendly *"Bonjour"* to the empty front room. If the poet is in a good mood she sings back to me, *"Bonjour, mignonne."* If I

am late or she has had a muscle cramp in her leg in the night and has been awake since before dawn she simply yells, *"Vite,* come quickly." In any case I enter her darkened bedroom and straighten out her legs.

"Avez-vous bien dormir?" I practice my French on her. She grumbles something about walking in her sleep. The radio is playing a lively polka. I pull back the curtains and lift the shades on the window facing the street, and the drab apartment is filled with pure, soft Paris light. She recites quickly and repeatedly in a voice hoarse with phlegm the poem she has spent the night arranging and rearranging in her head.

> *Do not weep for me*
> *I am stronger than a lioness*
> *protecting my heart from cruel truths.*
> *Do not linger at the well of pity,*
> *I drink bitter tears for wine.*

2. When the sun is spilling into the bedroom and she is relieved of the cramp in her leg, I lift her in three movements onto the portable toilet next to her bed to pee a long, loud stream that seems to go on forever. She has been holding her bladder since the Sister left at nine the night before. Sometimes she is unable to hold her water and the acrid smell of her piss nauseates me as I roll her from one side of the bed to the other to change her sheets and wipe down the rubber mattress cover with ammonia. I feel superior as she leans her frail body against mine, because I know that I can walk away from this

room and she never will. Edith Piaf, or someone who sounds like her, croons a sad love song on the radio.

3. I leave her sitting on the toilet and go into the kitchen to start her morning coffee. Two scoops of strong French roast boiled for five minutes, then strained into a small cracked Moroccan mug. The poet drinks it black with four sugars. I fry up one egg over easy and prepare one slice of dry wheat toast which I cut into four strips for dipping into the yellow eye of egg. When she yells my name I turn off the flame. There are stories I will write in my journal, but like the poet, I have been writing in my head because I am too exhausted at the end of the day to revisit my daily suffering.

4. I lift the poet off the toilet and into her wheelchair padded with lambswool and wheel her to the door of the bathroom, three feet away. I struggle to lift her onto the toilet in the tiny, dark cubicle. She sits drinking black coffee and smoking a cigarette craftily held between her almost lifeless fingers until her bowels move. She yells my name from the bathroom for me to come and wipe her ass. If her bowels are hard I give her more coffee or gently press her belly. She is like a little girl holding on to me, crying into my shoulder, uttering a sigh of sweet relief when her ordeal is over. Sometimes she says thank you, but it is a whisper, a gift.

5. I roll her out of the bathroom into the kitchen. She tries to eat her breakfast from a low shelf by the back door. The spoon in her hand flies around the plate and near her mouth. She chews slowly as she stares out at the wild garden of weeds be-

yond her door. I often wonder what she is thinking. What poems she imagines will let the world see what she sees, feel what she feels. When she is exhausted from trying to feed herself, she calls me over to finish feeding her the cold pieces of toast and egg left on her plate. I clean up the dishes from the night before while she watches me. I give her medication. Two green ones, a blue-and-white, three little yellows, or is it only one yellow and two big reds? I didn't intend to give her so many of the little yellow pills, but once I did, and she slept through lunch without bothering me once to take her for a piss or light her cigarette or wipe crust from the corners of her eyes. Sometimes I wish she would sleep forever. I want to finish a story I started long ago, but if I wrote it now, lies would mark the paper. In Paris I can tell any history that suits me.

"I have grown up into the kind of woman who wants to live fast and die young and handsome like my father, whom I love in spite of his sins."

I am reinventing myself so that everyone who looks at me will fall in love with the me they see.

6. I undress the poet Elizabeth and after a wrestling match I finally render her naked. She is a bag of sharp bones, a wrinkled leather suitcase with skin so hard in places she scratches me, so soft in other places I feel desire. I manage to slide her uncooperative body into the long, deep porcelain tub. I leave her there soaking in bubbles while I dust the knickknacks scattered all over the apartment. She shouts my name as if I couldn't hear the sound of sweat forming on her brow in the

tiny apartment. I stand outside the door to the bath counting to one hundred. I take a deep breath before I enter so that I don't say anything smart to make her mad. I soap a rough cloth and pass it over her neck and shoulders. I scrub her back, her lifeless arms, flaccid muscles. I pass the cloth over her long, thin breasts and inverted nipples, her small protruding belly, over her thighs, down her legs, her feet, between her toes. She likes to try to wash between her legs, but her limp fingers usually lose the cloth. With an embarrassed smile she lowers her eyes and offers her open legs to my hands. I am always tender, massaging the place between her legs with care. She still has feelings there. I can tell because she closes her eyes and tries to find a rhythm to ride my hand to a peaceful place. I manipulate her loose body like a puppet. Sometimes she comes violently against the rough cloth in my hand, her eyes closed, her mouth slightly open, gasping for breath. I direct her desire. Sometimes she whispers thank you, most times she looks away and lets her long upper body droop over her knees so that I can wash her narrow ass, its soft cheeks spread wide for my hand to enter. She may be in charge, but I am in control. My turn will come. I want the freedom to lose control. I want to be in love.

7. In her closet there are silver capes and feathered dresses of many colors. She has a story for each article of clothing. As if they have a personality and she does not. As if things happened to her clothes, not to her. She tells me about the night her black velvet hooded cape swept the floor at the ritzy La Coupole. The morning she found her red satin skirt hanging

from the chandelier in an Austrian couple's hotel suite at Le Crillon, her body sandwiched between man and wife. The week she lived in the white lace corset, her bare bottom spanked endlessly by her Hungarian lover's hand. She tries to scandalize me with her stories, but she forgets that I am not so innocent. I listen impassively to her fantasies.

After her bath, I dress her in large white cotton panties, a matching bra into which I fold her breasts. It is too difficult to zip and hook and tie delicate fabrics around her uncooperative body. I struggle to put her arms and shoulders into a faded pink shirt with broken buttons and her lifeless legs into a pair of pale blue knit slacks. She puts on her makeup. Eyes. Lips. Cheeks. Blue or green eye shadow and lipstick she rakes across her face too high or too low. Some days her hands do not cooperate at all. She always asks me to dab on her a bit of perfume, Poison, given to her by an old admirer.

"You must think I'm foolish, but it helps my morale," she says. "The doctor is coming today. If visitors call . . ." She hesitates. "I'm too depressed. Tell them I'm sleeping. Don't let them in. I don't want people to see me this way." She implies that I do not count as a person, my blackness shields her from shame. I am allowed to see her real true self. She thinks I don't feel anything, but I do.

8. When she is dressed I push her wheelchair into the front room next to the open window, where she can see the street sweepers and the cemetery wall next to the church and the trees peeking over it and a bit of sky. She interviews a new poet's helper for weekends, who arrives just as I did two

months before with all the expectations of assisting a great poet, and the poet Elizabeth is just as charming and cunning as she was with me. Her new girl, a slender fair-haired Swede, Brigitta, will start tomorrow.

9. She gives me money to go shopping, I am glad to smell fresh air again. I smile at shopkeepers and children on bikes giving them my best *"Bonjour."* I go to the butcher for liver and to the market for lemons and soap and to the bakery for bread. I buy a pack of cigarettes for her and one for myself at the *tabac* on the corner with the change left over. It isn't the same as stealing, she doesn't pay me what I'm worth. I inhale her secondhand smoke all day and get none of the pleasure. I start smoking again because the French make it look sexy and intellectual. My first cigarette in years makes me feel high. I can see my thoughts in the white column of smoke. I can see the ocean in my mind's eye.

10. While I prepare lunch she watches TV. I can hear it from the other room. A Pan American Airlines flight has been hijacked. Fifteen people are dead. A Palestinian group has claimed responsibility for the action. In Istanbul a group of armed men entered a temple during services and opened fire on worshippers. The dying were doused with gasoline and set on fire. Terrorism is murder with a message. Every day I walk the streets of Paris, aware that I could be blown apart by a bomb for a cause, good or bad. I am not afraid to die, because I am living, really living, not wondering what living would be like. Sometimes with the poet I feel like a hostage. But I need the slave wages she pays me so I can get

my own little room somewhere so that I can begin to write my own stories. The terrorists have a plan. I need a plan.

"Fou. Tout le monde. The whole world is crazy," she says. "Why should I want to live?" I too wonder why she clings to life so desperately, imagining after each session with her overenthusiastic, slightly disheveled East Indian physical therapist that she is improving, that she will walk again. Her disease has no cure. She will always be a poet. She will always need hands and legs, not her own, to help her through what is left of her life.

The hour I take for lunch, feeding her one mouthful and myself one from two chipped dinner plates balanced on my lap, she deducts from my pay. She says my lunch is free, but we both can see the lie in this. The piece of sautéed liver drizzled with lemon sits like a lump in my throat. It is hard for me to watch her drool and chew so slowly and swallow my own food at the same time.

11. Sometimes we play sad music. Albinoni's *Adagio,* Alison Moyet's *The Power of Love.* Sometimes I read poetry to her, and she recites from memory Baudelaire's erotic poems. I feel like her lover when she asks me to dry her tears.

"I used to teach poetry in a girls school outside of London. They were as eager as you are to create masterpieces of literature. I'll tell you the same secret I told them: No teacher can teach as well as the careful study of one great poem." Her favorite poets are Robert Frost, Edna St. Vincent Millay, and Baudelaire. She quotes sonnets and villanelles dramatically in the quiet afternoon, and her breath brings them to life. Her voice is delicate yet distinct, with a strength she doesn't appear to have.

One day she asks me what I want out of life.

I say, "Everything," then stop because there is a story she needs to tell.

"Be careful what you ask for. When I was young I was the tallest girl around. I towered over the tallest boy in my class. I used to wish I could cut off my legs. Now I'm trapped in this wheelchair, my legs effectively cut off. As a young girl I wasn't unlike other young girls. I wanted desperately to be married. I can't say I was in love, except with the idea of marriage. Everyone warned me vaguely about the doctor to whom I was engaged. Even his mother warned me, on our wedding day. That night in his parents' country house he left my bed and went to his lover's room down the hall. I stood outside the door listening to them and cried the whole night long. I looked through the keyhole and saw him lying next to the man who had been best man at our wedding. Still, for five years I tried to be a wife to him. But I just couldn't compete with his other life." Remembering, she begins to cry as if he has just left the room. She needs me. This is when I like her most, when I really savor being a poet's helper. When I feel my power to comfort or injure with a word or a backhand snap of my wrist. I am choosing to comfort. I dry her tears and mine with the same cloth. I hold her in my arms like a child, rock her close to my chest, and let her cry away all the memories.

"Don't be frightened of losing your innocence, that is what will free you," she says. "At night when the street sweepers come, I think about dying. I think about all the things I'll never do. All the places I'll never go, the people I'll never meet. My pillow is soaked by morning." She sleeps, and I dream of a time when she could walk into a room and decorate it with her beauty.

12. "St. Paul de Vence," she says quietly as if she has been reading my mind. "He lives there with his lover. Remember me to him. Baldwin is the most intelligent Negro I have ever met in my life. I hope that he is kind to you." She blows smoke out of the open window and gazes longingly at the cemetery wall. She's known all along why I've stayed. She's kept me here by sweet talking, cursing, and threatening me, and now she has given me the thing I've wanted all along. She knows she could not hold me here forever. "I knew you'd leave. I want you to remember me kindly, as I will remember you."

13. It is my last day as the poet's helper. After I've dusted every corner, mopped the floors, and cleaned the tiny kitchen, I place a blanket over the poet's lap. She is asleep in her chair by the window. Her head leans forward, chin to chest, her arms are limp, open palms upturned at her side. She looks like a cast-off rag doll. I lock the door to the apartment and shut the tall black gate behind me. I hurry because I don't want to be late to pick up the twins. I wonder if they'll cry when it's time for them to leave Paris. I wonder if they'll miss me.

I walk half a block west, and two blocks south, retracing my steps of the morning, stumbling down the narrow streets, blind from crying. I walk away and I don't look back with my eyes. A light rain is falling.

In Paris all the houses have eyes that cry each time it rains.

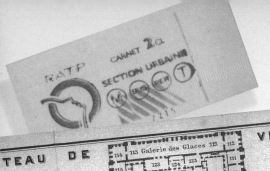

CHÂTEAU DE VERSAILLES

N
S

60 80 100
Mètres

114 113 Galerie des Glaces 113 112
115 123 124 125 111
116 126 110
117 121 120 127 129 109
118 130 128 108

Premier Etage (Aile du Nord)

(Aile du Midi)

140 142 107
144 143 106
105

Batailles 148 147 145
Sculpture 150

84 85 86 87 88 89 90 91 82 93 96
83 96 Galerie de Sculpture 96
98 100
99 101
104 103 102

Chapelle

48 49 50 51 Galerie basse 52 53 54
33 32 31 30 55
Cour de la Reine 34 29 Cour des Cerfs 56
45 28 Cour 57
44 Cour 27 158
43 59
42 25

Cour de Marbre

39 Cour Royale

Rez-de-Chaussée (Aile du Nord)

Vesti bule 1 2 3 4 5 6 7 8 9
16 Galerie de Pierre 16
Cour de 17 19 Cour du Maroc
18 20
21

Opéra Salle du Séna

(Aile du Midi)

73 72 71 70 69 68 67 66
74 81
Chambre des Députés
Cour du Nord
Cour des Princes

Wagner

lover

I HEARD HIM FIRST, so I couldn't say that Ving was good-looking to my eyes, but the sound of his horn made him forever handsome to my heart. He was the sound of a slow train leaving, a boat rocking in a stormy port, like something that could take you away or bring you home again. Before my eyes found him, I expected to see an old black man blowing, but Ving was far from that. He was forty then, but he looked to me like an overgrown little boy among the adults.

Do you know what it means to miss New Orleans . . . ?

The music was a strong rope pulling me through the crowded garden, toward him and those dark, blue, familiar notes.

He was pulling me home again with his blues.

His long, dark, curly hair was pulled back into a fluffy pony-tail. He wore thick, black-framed glasses on his heart-shaped face. He held his shiny silver trumpet in the air and gestured with it as if blowing holes through the trees. He was tall, flush faced, and lean. He looked like he needed a good meal. His jeans were rumpled and his red wool sweater was unraveling at the wrists. His hiking boots marched softly in time to the music. Eyes closed, head down, then bobbing up again when he blew, he filled his lungs, then his cheeks with wind that he directed through the horn into disturbing sounds. I used to sing the blues like that, at night in smoky places, making old men cry and young women sway and sing along. I could feel his music and it made me miss home. When Ving opened them, his big glossy eyes seemed almost brimming with tears, and his dented lips were pushed out as if he was about to kiss someone.

Indego and Carmen argued all the way to Kenya and back. After a few days of her complaints about money and her end-less physical ailments he had returned to Paris until he found another invitation to winter in the sun. When Indego saw me walking past the American Bookstore, he invited me to David's monthly soirée. Artists of all kinds and those who just wanted to be near them came together on the first Sunday of every month in David's atelier near Parc Monceau to eat, drink, and talk politics. By the time we arrived it was just turning dark. In-dego pulled a small piece of paper from his breast pocket and squinted at the numbers on its creased surface. He carefully punched in the entrance code on the silver numeric pad bolted inside the arched doorway. The enormous red wooden door was carved with sea creatures. A narrow stone path cut sharply through a wild garden toward a pair of two-story lofts, each with a wall of windows. Our host used one of the upper lofts as a photography studio and lived downstairs, where the soirées were held. The floors were covered with large black futons, where his friends and friends of friends could stay a night or more if they were adventurous and could stand the noise of happiness. The second loft, at the back of the garden, was occupied by an ancient Hungarian count, who according to Indego spent all day sipping cognac in his bathtub. The count no longer paid rent, but David didn't have the heart to throw him out, since he had gambled all his money away.

Indego warned me to be careful of David. "He's kinky," he said with a grin, making an obscene gesture with his hands. It sounded like a challenge. I imagined that having sex with David would be only slightly more daring than having dinner with him. David was a barrel-chested, bearded lumberjack type from Minnesota with a deep, hearty laugh and a philosophical interest in the international politics of sex. He was friendly with everyone and made the sound of a large animal welcoming home its mate whenever he greeted someone he knew. He lived with Basil, a young, frail English poet, and Medea, a voluptuous Greek dancer and performance artist, who was dancing topless against the stone garden wall when we arrived. Indego said he slept with them both and anyone else who'd join them. David was standing at the top of the garden, and when I came near enough he grasped me in an enveloping bear hug that lifted me off my feet and whispered something I couldn't quite understand in my ear. His beard tickled me and I laughed. His smile was warm and wicked. He slapped the leather seat of his pants and winked down at me. Wrapping his thick arm around my waist he moved me through the crowd and Indego followed. I felt light in his arms. He introduced us to a small knot of trendy, well-dressed older women, who smiled politely, acknowledging us with slight nods. When David and Indego stepped away to get drinks, the women turned from me to continue their conversation in French. More than thirty people were gathered in the front garden, snapping their fingers and shaking bells as accompaniment to Medea's performance. Her long, gray-streaked hennaed hair fanned about her bare shoulders, her strong tanned arms waved in the air like long grass underwater. Her large breasts rolled back and forth across her chest. Her soft round belly trembled. A gold coin belt around her curvy waist jingled, and a long red silk skirt whipped around her thick legs as her bare feet stamped down the damp earth as if it were on fire. David was distracted by the sound of the coins and bells, and I watched him join Medea in the garden. He stripped off his shirt, exposing his huge hairy chest, and moved in circles around her like a big dancing bear.

Indego handed me a drink and gripped me by the elbow, and we walked on toward the house. Inside, a dozen or so young men who all looked like models were sitting, smoking, whispering in small groups along the steps of a wide oak staircase. They were lit by small white votive candles in the curve of each step. Glittering faces. Mascaraed eyes. Tinted lips, wet hair sculpted with styling gel. Their bodies cut sharp profiles in tight

T-shirts and tailored pants. The scent of clove cigarettes and perfume overwhelmed me. Their glamour dazzled me. They all were smoking and talking with their hands.

Indego held onto my elbow until we passed the staircase and the main room of the house. Noisy conversation rose and fell all around us. Most of the guests were speaking English, but I could hear French and Spanish mingled with flat American accents too. About twenty people were standing crowded together in a corner of the room, drinking red wine from plastic cups.

Indego tried to keep an eye on me, but he kept getting pulled into conversations and was soon in a heated discussion about the Ethiopian economic situation with a British architect who lived in Nairobi, and I was left alone. I tried to introduce myself to three French women dressed in slim black leather pants and white linen shirts, but they were interested only in the German painter who was trying to describe to them in his limited English how to buy an authentic Turkish carpet. I did meet a carpenter from Oklahoma, Polish refugees, a psychiatrist from Argentina, a painter from Costa Rica.

The sound of the horn stopped suddenly and I missed it. I pressed myself against the wall and made my way into the kitchen area to freshen my glass from an unlabeled gallon jug of wine on a table filled with bottles of alcohol. I heard a voice behind me.

"Ving," he said. As I turned around I almost splashed the front of his sweater with wine. Several drops hit the floor instead. He stretched out his hand for me to shake, and when I took it he held onto mine as if he was falling and needed me to lift him up.

I was staring into bright blue eyes. Something hard pressed into the top of my thigh, and I looked down and saw the silver horn dangling from the fingers of his other hand.

"Eden." I wiggled my fingers in his, but he didn't let go, and because his hand was firm, warm, I relaxed.

"Were you playing before?" I asked.

"You like jazz?" His accent was American. Southern.

"I like to listen to music I can dance to." I pulled my hand away from his and held my plastic cup of wine in both hands between us.

"What kind of music is that?"

"Tina Turner, Aretha, Smoky Robinson, Chaka Khan, you know . . . *soul* music," I said, twisting my hips and shifting my shoulders from side to side as if my body could hear James Brown on his knees singing "Baby Please."

"But jazz is soul music," he said. There was something deep and rich about Ving's music, and the way he said "soul" made me believe he had it. Ving put his dented lips to his horn and blew out something I could dance to.

"That's all right." I danced a few steps, and he waved his trumpet around me like a snake charmer. When I noticed people staring at us I stopped, and he made a romantic flourish with his horn. There was applause from the people behind us in the center of the room. I took a sip of wine to disguise my nervousness.

"If you heard Sonny Rollins play the sax, he'd change your mind. Have you been to the new dance club at Bastille?" Ving asked, picking at the loose threads at his wrist.

"It costs two hundred francs to get in."

"Two-fifty, but you get a free drink," he said as if this was a bargain.

"Any way you look at it, that's a lot of money. I could get a room for the night and a turkey dinner." I took another nervous sip of the tangy red wine and peeked at him over the edge of my cup. Was he asking me out on a date? I wondered if he could dance to soul music. Where I came from, blacks and whites didn't dance together. The white people I had seen dancing on TV seemed to be listening to a different beat, dancing to sounds that didn't have anything to do with the music.

"Don't be afraid of me."

"I'm not afraid," I said, but I was lying. "I don't know enough about you to be afraid."

"I'm forty years old. I was born in New Orleans on Louis Armstrong's birthday. My father was an architect. He died in a car accident when I was three. My mother was a Southern belle. She was crowned Miss French Quarter when she was sixteen and never worked another day in her life. She lives in the south of France with my sister. I don't eat pork, and I laugh in my sleep. I came to Paris to play for a friend's wedding ten years ago and I never left."

"Why did you stay?"

"I went to a gypsy and had my fortune told."

"Serious."

"I guess I was looking for a new note. A different way of being in the music."

"Did you find it?"

"I'm still looking, but I'm enjoying the search. What are you doing here?"

"I'm looking for Langston," I blurted out. I felt dizzy.

"You do know that Langston Hughes is dead."

"I know that," I said. "But James Baldwin isn't." The wine was making me hot. Sweat began forming on my upper lip.

"You know him?" He seemed interested.

"When I finished reading *Giovanni's Room* I felt like I knew him . . . like he knew me. Like he knew everything about loneliness and a lot about pain. His stories make me believe that what I know matters, but what I *do* is more important than anything else. Do you know him?"

"*Another Country, The Fire Next Time, Nobody Knows My Name.* He writes in the language of jazz. He plays the blues on a typewriter. You could say I know him. Jimmy was here in Paris a few months ago."

"You've met him?" Now I was interested.

"He comes to the club where I play sometimes. We had a few drinks, told some lies."

Indego was watching us from where he was holding court on the stairs. He motioned for me to come over, but I ignored him. Ving had hypnotized me.

"I'm writing a novel," I said.

This seemed to intrigue him.

"What's it about?"

"I don't know yet. I guess I'm kind of like you, looking for a new way to be in language, to bring life to words, to make stories real and important like Langston did, like Baldwin does."

I told him about working for the poet Elizabeth, cooking, cleaning, bathing and caring so much it hurt, and he understood why I was so tired. He seemed to understand why being in Paris was so important to me. He promised to help me find Baldwin. His face was incredibly sweet and soft.

"I'm tired, listening to your routine. You don't have much time to write, do you?"

I shook my head as if to clear my mind, took a deep breath, and tried to think of an excuse to leave the party. I was beginning to wonder what sense it had made to leave the comfort of home. Ving seemed to be listening to me, but his eyes roamed around the room. He acted as if he knew everybody, and nodded to people coming and going to the terrace outside, smoking cigarettes.

"Do you want to go listen to jazz sometime?" he asked, looking into the well of his horn.

I was stunned by his question, and it must have shown on my face. I had never been on a date with a white man. I was afraid, but I did want to know this man. I wanted to listen to his private music. I didn't say anything for a minute. I just stared at him as if he had hit me on the head with his horn.

When I was growing up in Georgia, young white boys and men in cars and pickup trucks drove through my neighborhood at night, stopping young black girls to ask if they wanted a ride. My father warned me that those men and boys meant us no good and that all most of the pickup girls had to show for their night rides were light-skinned babies and the distinction of being called niggers when the boys' parents or wives found out. They were raped and left by the side of the road when they were no longer useful. My father called these men white devils, and my mother said trust none but Jesus, and we prayed for the souls of white folks.

And then Ving began to shine, and when he looked at me his face flushed as if he'd been caught. His blue eyes shimmered.

"Yeah, why not," I said, sure my father in heaven would never find out about my betrayal.

Indego reached me, grabbing my arm, pulling me away from the devil.

"You're with me," Indego said, as if I belonged to him. I didn't resist, because I had made up my mind and Ving had offered me something I didn't want to resist.

Later in the evening Ving came up behind me and slipped his phone number into the pocket of my coat and walked away playing a lively New Orleans funeral march, and it was the music that made me decide to call him. I felt that another useless belief had died and that the road ahead of me was paved with new riches. I remembered that I was in Paris and there was no one to judge my actions, no one to remind me of my disloyalty to the race, to accuse me of losing my blackness, no one to remind me of the master-slave relationship. I was a free woman and could choose whom and what I wanted.

"Watch out for them musicians, you can't depend on them. They married to the music," Indego said, watching me watch Ving march out into the garden to serenade the male models, who had stripped down to stark white briefs. They were dancing together under a willow tree decorated with a string of lights that twinkled like real stars. I had never seen men dance together, but there in David's garden it seemed natural. They did not look wicked, they looked happy, and I was happy for them.

I didn't ask what Indego meant about musicians, I just followed him around until it was time to go back to my little room in the house where I was an au pair and sleep in a bed not my own, dreaming of a bed in which I could wake up without my body being on fire.

A few days after David's soirée I had an unexpected holiday. The children's school was closed for the day so that its broken heating system could be repaired. The mother offered to take the children to the zoo. Relieved and elated at my good fortune I took a bus to the Latin Quarter and walked along the quai St-Michel, near the hotel where I stayed my first night in Paris, mingling with the tourists. The Latin Quarter was like a village in many ways. I began to recognize familiar faces. Waiters in the little cafés I had gone to with Delphine remembered me. It was cloudy and raining lightly, but to me it was a beautiful day and all I had to do was daydream and look at the sights. On her days off the Welsh au pair used to follow American tour groups and blend in, making friends with older couples at the back of the group. She would often be asked to join them for meals and invited onto their large buses for tours of the countryside. I could not blend in so well. My skin marked me, set me apart even though I was the American.

I wanted something good to read, and I refused to go to the American Bookstore, where the ugly green suit might be waiting to humiliate me. Indego told me that sometimes the African booksellers had books in English by African Americans. I wondered if there were other books about the black artists' experience in Paris. If there was a guide. An African bookseller wearing a black knit cap pulled over his ears and a short, puffy black parka over a long white caftan shuffled in place, rubbing his hands together as if warming them over a fire. He greeted me with a broad smile, flashing beautiful teeth, one of which was solid gold. His eyes were interested in the more prosperous tourists who passed by his stall to jostle each other at the next stand for postcards of old Paris and French colonial scenes. I looked through the stacks of *Ebony* magazines encased in dusty plastic envelopes. I picked up a magazine with Dorothy Dandridge on the cover. She was so sexy and glamorous and she looked out at me as if offering me something wonderful. Out of the corner of my eye I saw a familiar face. Ving, the horn player, was talking to a tourist in front of the postcard stall. When he saw me he winked and tipped his horn in my direction. He finished his conversation with the tourist and moved toward me.

"Do you think it's raining in Algeria?" he asked, looking up at the sky. My ears were delighted by the sound of his English.

"Is African water wet?" I answered in code as if I were Mata Hari, a spy in the house of a stranger, waiting for a sign.

"Good answer." He smiled, and I bit my suddenly dry lips, aching for a word.

"I didn't get a chance to call you."

"You don't have to now." He walked with me across the bridge to a popular ice cream stand and bought a large cone with three flavors. We took turns eating it, licking the drips off our fingers. He talked jazz like most men I'd known talked sports or cars. Miles Davis, John Coltrane, Charlie Parker, Lester Young, Coleman Hawkins, King Oliver, and his musical godfather, Louis Armstrong. Most of the names meant nothing to me. He talked about these men as if he knew them, as if they were part of his family. They had taught him about life, he said. He knew things because of them. He knew other important things, like how airplanes stayed in the sky, and he knew philosophy and literature and geography and history. He read Greek plays for fun. He was full of information and kept his heart where I could see it. He wanted to know everything about me, and when I told him, he listened as if my story were the most important in the world. He kept a respectful distance but let me know he would like to come closer when I was ready.

I couldn't turn away from the sound of Ving's voice. When he talked about jazz it sounded as if he was talking about sex. He bought a book of French poetry and we sat on a park bench, where he read to me from Baudelaire's *Les Fleurs du Mal*. I didn't understand the poems in French, but Ving made them sound like romantic love songs. He translated one of the poems for me. "A Une Dame Creole," "To a Creole Woman." Written as a compliment to an exotic island beauty, the poem stated that if she came to Paris, her beauty would inspire sonnets in the hearts of poets, making the French even more submissive than her island blacks.

Later, on the phone, Ving talked to me about sex all night long. His words made me want to come. I whispered with him in the dark after I was done for the day being a poet's helper and an au pair. I sat in the TV room in my nightgown at the card table by the blue light of the mute TV. I was pudding when he softly said words like "pussy" and "fuck." For days all we did was talk. *He tells me what to do to my body in the blue light and I do it.* I slid my body onto the floor under the table and I touched myself. His breathing was deep and steady, soothing. I waited. He was the conductor and my body an entire orchestra.

One finger. Now two.

"What do you smell like? What do you taste like?" he whispered.

I came only when he told me to.

"Are you with me?" he breathed, taking care not to rush the moment.

"Yes." I twisted the phone cord around my wrist, waiting patiently to see how far we would go this time.

On Sunday after the family had left for a picnic in the country, I invited Ving to the apartment. He arrived with a bottle of red wine and a small gold box of chocolates. I closed the door to my little room, and we lay on the carpet in front of the tall open window. The view of the sky was half-obscured by bare-limbed trees. The wine was dry and tasted like cherries. The chocolates were filled with a dark rich mousse. Ving pushed my shirt up over my stomach. He melted one of the little chocolates by rubbing it across my bare belly, then took a sip of wine and licked the chocolate off my skin. He made little sucking noises and tickled me with his breath.

"Let me touch you," he said softly. And he did with good intentions, but his hands were large and clumsy.

"Kiss me there." I pointed to my chest.

I tried to focus on his tongue, soft, wet, and dangerously close to engulfing me. It snaked and glided across the broken places. Suddenly his mouth was full of my breast. I tried to speak, to give him more commands, but I couldn't. There were no words to tell him what I wanted, and even then I wasn't sure he would understand. I wanted tenderness and whispers, rough talk and a little pain. I wanted to feel something deep inside of me, pushing to the other side. Shifting my body above his, I slow danced on his lap. I was afraid to need something so much. I was terrified. I pushed against him, slowly guided him inside me.

"Hold me," he said.

I leaned forward and I took him in my arms and held him. I took a holiday from my body. I became someone else. I watched impassively as the white stream of his cum soaked into the carpet.

When I walked through the park after being with Ving, a new feeling hung in the air around me. On a quiet street under the leaves of a plane tree, love became a possibility. I wanted to tell somebody how new I felt.

Days spent cooking and cleaning for the children and looking after the poet passed in a blur. One Saturday night, after I walked the dog and put the children to bed, I took the métro to Montparnasse to meet Ving at his apartment. We had a date to hear a live jazz concert. Ving told me that he lived down the street from one of Picasso's studios and around the block from the eighteenth-century *maison* where Balzac wrote and hid from his creditors. Ving's place was on the third floor of an old, well-kept building, in a back courtyard. The one-bedroom apartment had a full bath with hot and cold running water. I pushed open the huge door and entered the quiet courtyard. I crossed the clean-swept atrium and entered the hallway of the building. I pressed the light switch, but before I could reach the third floor the light went out and I was surrounded by pitch blackness. I pressed myself against the cracked plaster wall and slowly made my way up the next floor. Food odors were strong. Garlic and onions seemed to sizzle in the air. I walked carefully up the narrow winding staircase.

"Eden?" I heard my name being whispered in the darkness from the floor above. "Follow the sound of my voice. I'm here." Ving was standing in the doorway of his apartment with a big smile on his face.

"I found you," I said, and we hugged each other in the darkness.

Inside Ving's apartment there were books and records everywhere. One entire wall was a floor-to-ceiling built-in bookcase. Framed black-and-white photographs of musicians from Paris in the Fifties lined another of the crisp white walls. The lighting was low, and a lamp shaded by antique lace gave off a yellowish glow. He offered me a drink, but I declined. My hands were shaking. I sat on the sofa and watched him pull his hair back into a ponytail with a rubber band. He wrapped a scarf around his neck and slipped into a navy blue wool peacoat. He took both my hands and pulled me up off the sofa and suddenly we were standing so close we could have kissed. I wanted to. My body hesitated. I looked into the flame of his blue eyes and saw something tender there. I slid my arms around his waist and laid my head on his chest. I could feel his heart beating. His arms wrapped around me, and we stood like that, holding each other as if we could delay an important decision.

"Don't you think we should get married?" He sounded serious, but he couldn't be.

"I don't know anything about you," I said into his chest.

"I told you everything about me that was important the first time I met you."

"Not statistics. Tell me a secret," I said. "Something you've never told anyone before."

A quiet mist seemed to settle over the room. Ving pulled me down to the floor, and we sat with our backs against the sofa, our eyes looking at the blank wall in front of us as if the images of his life were rolling against it. I leaned into his side, let him hold me close.

"I used to dress up in my sister's clothes."

I tried to imagine him in a dress, and it wasn't so hard. In some ways he was soft like a woman, gentle, pretty. We blinked and kept looking at the wall, trying to see what was in front of us.

"It must've been fun playing dress-up," I said twisting a lock of his long hair around my finger.

"Yeah, it was fun." He sounded sarcastic. He started picking at the nap in the carpet, then crossed his arm over his chest.

"Doesn't sound like fun. Did you get caught?" I giggled, stroking the thick veins on the inside of his wrist.

He hesitated, then curled up beside me. His arm was heavy across my belly. He smelled like smoke, oranges, and wine. I was sorry I laughed. I stroked his hair, kissed the top of his head. He became sober, serious, almost too heavy to hold in my arms. His words were like stones he laid at my feet. *I have become wet earth for stories like these, they take root in me and grow wild, nearly choking me.*

"Every summer my sister went to visit relatives in the south of France. I went to the baby-sitter's house in the mornings, but I spent the afternoons wearing my sister's dresses. Flowered ones with puffed sleeves, simple shifts, and velvet jumpers with bows. My mother caught me after I'd done it only a few times, but she wasn't upset. She said it was our secret. One day she took me shopping for my own dresses. She kept them locked in a suitcase in a corner of the attic. Every summer my mother called me Marie. She plaited ribbons in my hair and bathed me every night in warm milk. She was very affectionate with me and held me like this, but she touched me there. She touched me there."

His tears stained the carpet like blood. I turned to him, attempted to protect him from waves crashing all around us. He crawled inside me, attaching himself to my lungs, my liver, my heart. He was hard, and once he was inside me we rocked back and forth. We made love slowly, tenderly on the floor, in the dim light. My body sucked poison from him and he found relief.

I was not prepared for that kind of secret. My stomach knotted as if I had been the one hurt. I wanted to take it back, make everything all right, but I knew that would be useless.

"I'm sorry," I said, not knowing what else to say.

"You didn't hurt me."

"Do you still see her?" I was hoping his mother was dead. His pain was still visible on his skin.

"I haven't for a long time. Years. I don't want to talk about her any more."

"Do you want to stay here?" I stroked his back. His fingers traced the outline of my ears, my face and neck.

"I think we'd better go," he said, pulling away.

We dressed in the dim light and moved around the room in silence with the mean secret between us. I kept hold of his right hand, and we walked like that, my brown hand in his pale one, to the boulevard to catch a taxi to the other side of town, and the world did not swallow us up.

The Roxy was packed. A line wrapped around the block. The names of three musicians whom I'd never heard of were emblazoned on the marquee. Sonny Rollins was the headliner. Ving took my arm and led the way to the front door, pushing a path for us. At the front of the line he flashed a press pass one of his journalist friends had loaned him, and suddenly we were inside the glittering lobby and up the red-carpeted stairs and leaning back into dark plush balcony seats in a theater packed with more than five hundred people. When the house lights dimmed Ving took my hand and put it in his pocket.

The first note startled me. A sharp, long, winding thread of sound that stretched far beyond my notions of the limits of music. The second note danced, the third made me want to stand up and shout. Sonny Rollins played the sax like Mahalia sang gospel like John Lee Hooker sang the blues like a preacher prayed on Sunday, with true devotion. I became a believer. This was soul music. My eyes were wet from crying. I was grateful to the messenger. I turned and kissed Ving on his cheek. I had found a new spice on an undiscovered island in my very own sea.

After the concert we walked along the quai. Moonlight was reflected in the Seine. The water looked like blue ink.

"I feel like I've been to church. I want to write like that," I said.

"You'll do it too. When you get your room to write," he said.

"This is what I feel when I read Baldwin. Like I've found my original language." I could still taste the music.

"When I met Baldwin he said he really dug my music, that it reminded him of the old-school guys he listened to when he was young. 'You got talent,' he said, 'but you sound like too many other people. You've got to make the music yours. Tell your own story with the horn.' "

"What was he like?" I asked.

"Baldwin? The night I met him in the nightclub he drank a lot, laughed and told stories, repeated his favorite ones, but you never got tired of listening. He wasn't as angry as his books. He wasn't angry at me for being white, like I thought he would be. I think he is a king. He lives in the south. In Nice or some-place near Cannes. I can't remember. He said the city had too many distractions. He lives in a little village down there. The guy who owns the club where I met him would know. I'll ask." Even though I had Baldwin's address—I'd earned it working for the poet—I didn't know if I'd have the courage to use it. I wanted him to discover me. What would happen if I burst through the hedges and knocked on his door, interrupting his work or disturbing his sleep? I was so close and so afraid that I would get what I wanted after all. I wanted someone to intro-duce me to him and I hoped that he would be kind.

Under a streetlight I kissed Ving, spontaneously, just be-cause I could, and he kissed me back. His kisses were eager, pas-sionate. I was drunk with the jazz, the kisses, and the fresh night air, and hope was in me.

One of Ving's best friends was a Haitian drummer named

Olu-Christophe, a handsome man in his thirties with velvety brown skin and enormous eyes. His face was a map of Africa. He played the talking drum as if possessed. Sweat streamed down his face in little rivers, his wiry arms flying, his hands moving so fast I could hardly see them. He had been a medical student in Haiti, sent to Paris eight years before to further his studies, but his family told him not to return because the government had been harsh to students returning from abroad. They were said to be agitators and suspected Communists. Many were jailed or killed with little evidence. The nearly thirty-year reign of the self-proclaimed Presidents for Life, François and Jean-Claude Duvalier, had ended earlier in the year, but Olu-Christophe was still afraid to go home. He made money playing with Ving. Sometimes he played the métro, and had been sending money home over the years. More than once he had threatened to kill Jean-Claude Duvalier and burn the bones of his father. We had dinner together one night in a Chinese restaurant near Les Halles. Olu-Christophe told us horror stories about life under a dictatorship. He said he had a plan to raise the quality of life for all Haitians. His eyes turned hard and cold, and he didn't speak again for the rest of the meal.

One night, Ving, Olu-Christophe, and I strolled along arm in arm to a club in the basement of a hotel on a side street in Bastille. Only ten or twelve tables. A five-piece band. When we entered the club, a sweaty Spaniard with jet black hair and black eyes that looked like sparkling jewels and the whitest, most perfect teeth I have ever seen was onstage. King Rain was what Ving's friend called himself, Ving called him Omar the Spaniard. He looked like a poor imitation of an Elvis imper-

sonator in his pale blue leather jumpsuit, twisting and howling
Seventies pop tunes into a microphone while two skinny white
girls, one of whom was his very pregnant Russian girlfriend,
gyrated in the background. The women wore garish glittery
makeup, their hair teased high on their heads, their bodies
squeezed into short, tight, gold tube dresses and their feet into
shiny white patent leather boots. I was shocked to see Omar's
girlfriend do a split—her big belly looked like a golden bubble
rising from the floor in front of her. After King Rain and his
Golden Girls ended their first set they came over to sit with us.
Ving bought drinks for everybody at the table. Olu-Christophe
flirted with the women. They all spoke English. Ving toasted
his friend's opening-night success. They passed around a cigarette I soon realized was hashish. It smelled sweet and made me
a little nauseous. I suddenly thought I could speak French and
managed a fractured conversation with an Arab journalist who
didn't speak English at all. Perhaps I was hallucinating, but we
seemed to be discussing modern-day slavery in Sudan. We
talked to each other, absorbed in our tangle of languages, for
what seemed like an hour. The DJ played salsa and merengue,
reggae and Afro pop. When James Brown started singing
"Papa's Got a Brand-New Bag," Ving pulled me up out of my
seat and onto the dance floor, where he showed me just how
much soul he had. His hips were fluid and his feet knew the
rhythms well.

"Surprised?" he asked, shifting his shoulders and swiveling
his hips like a son of James Brown.

"Truth?"

"Truth."

"You sure about your grandmother?"

"Sure about what?"

"How you got that dark curly hair in New Orleans. You sure there's no smoke in your fire? You could be my distant cousin. I'm an orphan, you know." He smiled and hugged me to him. Ving asked me if I wanted to go to his apartment. I whispered yes and kissed him softly on the ear. I wanted him to fuck me. This thought surprised me, then made itself at home. I wanted him to bury himself inside me and rock-and-roll me and jazz me and moan and turn me blue and aquamarine and sink and sink and light me up from the inside. I wanted to turn him out, ruin him, make him forget all the women he ever knew before me. Forget the pain his mother caused him. My body itched against his like a cat in heat.

It was almost one o'clock in the morning when Ving and I left the club. Olu-Christophe had made friends with the single Golden Girl and left with her around midnight. Ving and I were hot and sweaty from dancing. Ving took his hair down and shook it out around his shoulders. He looked like a handsome girl. I touched his hair, then took his hand. We left our coats open and walked out into the cool night air. We walked hand in hand past several bars, toward the métro. A few blocks from the club it felt colder and I shivered. He slipped his arm around my shoulder and pulled me close. He was warm and I felt safe and new in his arms. For a few moments, the world was all right. Then the piss in the gutter began to stink. My body stiffened against Ving's as we approached a group of four young men drinking beer from bottles in front of a crowded bar. They were arguing loudly in French. The group grew quiet as we passed them. Ving didn't seem to notice, but I started to sweat and walked a little faster.

One of them spoke loud enough for us to hear. I could make out a few French words. *T'as vu, le pédé qui promène son chien noir.* Look at the queer walking his black dog. *Salope. Putain.* Bitch. Whore. They were yelling at our backs. *Salope. Putain.* Bitch. Whore. When we were only a few steps from the métro stairs a beer bottle crashed against the sidewalk a few feet in front of us. Another one flew like a missile past the left side of my face. I didn't look back. We ran down the stairs into the subway and jumped the turnstile. My heart was beating like an overworked motor. We stood on the platform shaken and scared, listening for the sound of footsteps that did not come. When the train arrived we entered the empty car and sat in silence, not touching. I was still frightened. I wanted to erase the past few minutes, but I couldn't. *Salope. Putain. Chien noir.* My libido was gone. I didn't want to have sex at all.

"Are you okay?"

I nodded, but I wasn't.

"Bastards. Stupid kids." He tried to lighten our load, but it was still too heavy to bear. Not far enough away to escape a familiar kind of humiliation. No translation was necessary.

"Everybody not free, somebody somewhere is a nigger tonight." My father's words blazed in my memory. Those men hadn't cared that I was American, college-educated, and Christian; all they saw was the color of my skin. Back home, I still wouldn't be able to hold Ving's hand without inviting comment or threat. What made me think I could be free? He was a white man, yet he couldn't protect me here in Paris or any part of the world. What kind of future could we have together? What about our children, if we had any? If I'd had a gun I would've killed somebody. My sweet high was gone.

We were alone in the métro car for the whole ride. The train passed my stop. We got off at Montparnasse and walked down the long deserted blocks to his building. His apartment was dark and cold inside. He lit a candle and cursed when he bumped into a stack of books. He plugged in a small electric heater, put water on to boil, and poured me a cup of hot green tea. He avoided touching me. I avoided his eyes and the secrets I would never tell. Ving wasn't upset when I asked if he would give me covers so that I could spread out on the couch cushions. He tried once more to kiss me, and I let him, but after pushed him away gently without explanation. He watched me curl up under the covers, then bent over and kissed me on my forehead. He pulled the covers up around my neck and put out the candle.

"Sweet dreams," he said. I turned my back to him and cried myself to sleep in the dark. I tried to remember that Ving was not the one who had hurt me, but all I could do was cry.

When I woke up I was cold and could hear Ving in the kitchen, feet shuffling in Italian leather slippers sent by his mother. I could smell the rich aromas of strong Turkish coffee and day-old bread toasting in the broiler. When he came into the room I reached up and put my arms around his neck and kissed his scratchy cheek until I smelled the bread burning. We pretended we had forgotten the other pain, the thing that had grown between us the night before.

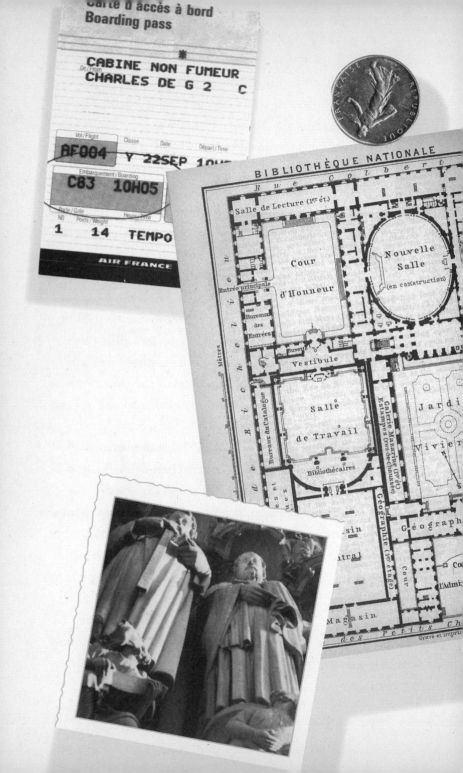

english teacher

PROFESSOR MAY DAY'S Sunday sit-downs were famous and sometimes met on Monday.

> *Take rue St Jacques past the Sorbonne. Cross boulevard St-Germain and the length of the open market. Walk up the hill past the fish market. When you come to the Greek restaurant on the left, go past it. Turn right into what looks like an alley. Cross the courtyard, enter the foyer in the center, and walk up five flights. The apartment on the left is the one you're looking for. Leave your shoes on the Oriental mat. Knock three times and touch the silver mezuzah for good luck.*

Olu-Christophe took me to my first sit-down. He knew I was homesick. I had called home only once, to let my mother know

I'd arrived safely. I was waiting to write a letter home that would tell Mama and Aunt Victorine about large victories. Olu-Christophe promised me that a visit to the Professor would cure me.

"Does the Professor believe in voudou like you?" I said, teasing him.

"No voudou, no magic," he said. "Just soul food and black people."

"Wish I could come for some of that soul food," Ving said, knowing he wasn't invited.

"I'll give you some soul food when I come back." I kissed him, and he held me close.

"You have places to go. I'll take care of the lady," Olu-Christophe said.

Ving and I blew kisses at each other as we went our separate ways. Olu-Christophe kept his eyes on the wet pavement as we walked. His shoulders were rounded and he walked like an old man, carrying his drum at his side.

"Are you maybe a little bit homesick too?" I asked.

He was silent. We walked for several blocks before he spoke.

"I miss my family, the food, speaking my language. I miss everything. When I first arrived in Paris I was insulted and harassed when I said I was Haitian. People called me dirty, accused all Haitians of having AIDS. Sometimes I pretended to be French or African. There was so much turmoil and corruption and fear at home. I was trapped between two places and couldn't live in peace in either one."

Olu-Christophe had tried to find peace by becoming an assassin. When the Duvalier family fled Haiti after thirty years of a murderous dictatorship and having stripped the nation's treasury of millions of dollars, they were granted asylum in France. For a while they lived in a villa on the edge of Paris, protected by a large contingent of French police. Olu-Christophe went there once and watched the house and waited for an opportunity to kill Jean-Claude and Michele Duvalier. He saw one of their children at the window for a moment before someone snatched it away. He said he was patient, he would wait, and one day he would kill them all. He did not look like an assassin. He looked lost and far away from home. I didn't believe he could kill someone, but the horrors he described made me wonder if I wouldn't feel the same if I were him.

Professor May Day's every gesture was dramatic. No audience was disappointed. You could almost see flashes of inspiration in the shine of his waxy bald head. He was tall and portly, but his movements were birdlike, quick and animated. He was a rare breed. He had been a musician playing his tarnished saxophone and quoting Sixties poetry in the Latin Quarter in his youth. A battered beret was left open-mouthed and hungry at his feet. His poetic jazz novel sold hundreds of thousands of copies in the early Sixties, and after traveling around the world for years, he settled in Paris, renting three rooms above a Greek restaurant. He hadn't published anything since because now he was living his novels. He and Indego were as different as East and West. They knew each other and had often read together, but their styles were opposite. An eccentric host, Professor May Day greeted his guests in a rich Mississippi baritone and gave each of us our name for the evening. *Melt Down, Homegrown, Dude. Flat Top, Black Top, Love Letter, Blues.*

Guests arrived around two in the afternoon with food of-ferings wrapped in waxed paper bags. On the Sunday after-noon that Olu-Christophe took me to my first sit-down at Professor May Day's, Miles Davis's trumpet was blowing. Sev-eral fat orange cats lounged lazily on the windowsills. A poet from Cameroon brought miniature puff pastries, *Melt Down;* slices of ham and a bottle of red wine from the black American painter living at Cité des Arts on a Fulbright, *Homegrown;* Olu-Christophe brought a bottle of wine and his drum, *Dude;* the el-egant brother from Guadalupe, *Flat Top,* brought his battered saxophone; the sculptor from Mexico, *Black Top,* brought cheese; a blind woman in an orange dress, *Love Letter,* held a ripe tomato in her hand; I brought two baguettes. *Blues.*

Professor May Day had covered an old army trunk with a threadbare Turkish carpet and set a big black enamel teapot in the center and a dozen little black cups without handles around it. There were delicately painted Japanese bowls, smooth, dark wood spoons and a pot of butter for the grits that bubbled in a huge metal pot on a hotplate by the window. Grits, Professor May Day said, were especially for the homesick black Ameri-cans. Northerners were offered sugar for their grits, yellow cheese for the Southerners, hot sauce for the Texans. Stewed okra gumbo was served on days particularly homesick for Pro-fessor May Day. Strong coffee and bottles of wine stood by to wash it all down. Food was eaten at various points during the sit-down.

That particular Sunday, after everyone had introduced himself, Professor May Day opened the gathering with a sermon on the government support of artists.

"Artists are part of a nation's treasure. America is the richest nation on the planet," he began solemnly. "Now don't you think they could support they artists. Hell no. There's the crime. I believe it's simple, we talking basic rights here. The U.S. government could support its cultural warriors by giving them free or subsidized housing and money to live on."

"I believe that there is subsidized housing for artists in New York," the painter, Homegrown, interjected.

It being his first time he was unaware of the seriousness of interrupting the flow of the mighty tide. Professor May Day almost jumped out of his chair shouting at breakneck speed, veins bulging in his shiny temples.

"I'm talking about across the board for every artist everywhere with the courage to create something meaningful, not just in New York. I'm talking about free medical, free materials, and a grant you could live on for say ten years or until your income reaches a certain level. I ain't saying something for nothing. Look at Sweden. The government buys work from the artist. They take care of them. For a monthly income or housing an artist could do a number of years of community service part-time. Teach in schools, workshops, or be commissioned to write music or design visual arts for the community. This is what I'm talking about. A community could commission a composer to write a score for their local orchestra. Installation art at the old folks home. The possibilities for non-artists to see how their tax dollars can support creativity are endless. Just like doctors get them government grants to go to medical school and they work it off in public service. Now I'm the last one to work for the silly ass U.S. government, but you really be working for the people. Art is just as important as food, 'cause if your soul ain't nourished, you one empty mutherfucker. That's one of the reasons I live here. Now the French government take care of they national treasures. French people think somebody crazy enough to choose the life of an artist and commit to it deserve to be supported. They appreciate art and creativity. Only reason I ain't got no French passport is that it is entirely too dangerous to do so. My papers in order and yours better be. This ain't no paradise. They kicking black asses back to Africa fast as you can blink. I can go places on Uncle Sam a French passport wouldn't take me. Now y'all come on get these cheese grits and eat them before they get cold." Then he took several deep breaths and spread his arms wide in a gesture of welcome.

The grits were smooth, rich with butter and fresh cream. A bowl of grated cheddar cheese was passed with the reverence of holy communion. I was at once grateful for the aroma and ashamed of my tears. I could hardly swallow for the lump in my throat. I missed my mother's arms. Wondered what Aunt Vic would be doing on a Sunday after church. Probably working a quilt with the sisters of Modern Miracles or cooking dinner for the minister or eating by herself at the big, empty dining room table. Each week I sent a postcard to Mama and Aunt Vic to let them know I was alive. They sent letters to the American Express Office. I would call again soon to hear the sound of their voices, but I would wait until I was sure I wouldn't start to cry because I was feeling like such a failure without a job, a regular place to live, or a good start on my writing.

"I have some pictures to show," the painter said. He unzipped an expensive leather portfolio and began to pass around small oil-painted canvases, all of the same image—crudely shaped hearts with odd little houses in the center.

"What the hell you want to say?" Professor May Day demanded.

"I'm exploring the strength of latent images in a complex series of imaginary elements inherent in a . . ."

"He just miss his mama," somebody said.

"Or his mama's cooking." We laughed.

"Speak clearly, man. If your audience have to dig too deep, where is the incitement to riot? You don't have to condescend to make it plain," Professor May Day boomed.

"Well, that's one way of looking at it. I want to challenge my audience . . ."

"I see what you saying. You got a good rap, but your work must stand on its own. You are not going to be standing in the gallery to explain all that shit. Remember that."

Professor May Day liked playing devil's advocate, insisting that out in the world one would have to defend one's art. He was often contradictory, sometimes illogical, but that was the piece of theater he thrived on. Strict attention was paid when someone was presenting or performing. Attention did not mean silence, for works of excellence were praised much as a sermon in a Southern Baptist church on Sunday would be. Call and response. Africa to the Americas and the Caribbean. *Teach, Preach, Word. Shout outs.* Then there was music. The talking drums, flying dreads, the bright alto sax. The blind woman dancing in a tight circle, her bright orange dress swishing left and right. Her thin charcoal arms raised to the sky. Heads rocked, spoons and hands beat thighs in personal time. When the energy in the room subsided I read my poem.

> *A generous pinch of educated ground African red pepper*
> *2 raw eggs from a Socialist chicken*
> *12 Spanish Separatist raisins*
> *27 grains of salt from the Red Sea*
> *& 8 stingy strips of green and Gold Coast peppers*
> *Make a bloody omelette.*
> *5 homemade bombs*
> *18 machine guns*
> *437 bodies and 300,000 screams in the middle of the day*
> *and every single night*
> *Make a bloody war.*

For a while there was silence, then a few "amen"s. Professor May Day started talking about the old days in Paris, when he knew Langston.

"Langston lived for a time at the Hotel California. His physical beauty was marred only by his rotten teeth. He couldn't afford to have them fixed. Take care of your teeth," Professor May Day said, then read a few poems by Langston.

Professor May Day led the discussion on local and world events. Gossip and hometown happenings were allowed if available and interesting.

"Says in the paper here, and you can believe what you want to, that more than a hundred Africans, from Mali, was deported. Says here some of them was so scared of going back they stripped buck naked and lay down on the runway."

Olu-Christophe tapped on his drum.

"If I went home to Haiti it would mean a certain death. I love my country. It is a terrible thing to be in exile, so far from home, among people who do not understand the horror of living under a dictator. Someday I feel all of us who are in exile will go home again. I still wear the key to my mother's house on a string around my neck. When we first came here I expected to return shortly, and I thought everything would be the same. My bicycle in the yard, my father in the garden, and my mother preparing food for us. Because I have become a man in this country my eyes are no longer veiled. I know that a change must come before I return, and nothing will ever be the same. Too much blood has been spilled."

Tap tap, tap tap tap . . . Tap-tap, tap tap tap . . .

"The French in it as deep as the Americans and a lot of other Western countries supporting dictatorships. They help create the mess, then don't want to clean it up. When the Ayatollah Khomeini left Iran with blood on his hands, where did he find a home? France. When the Duvaliers left Haiti with bags of blood-soaked money, where did they go? To the French Riviera. Immigrants ain't nothing new. Lots of folks come here in the Fifties from former French colonies to do work the French didn't want to do. Street sweepers, maids, and nannies. Folks started bringing they families over here and having babies. Born in France, born French. Now that the population is swelling, the French making new laws to keep immigrants out and deny citizenship to them that's born here. They created all this mess with colonization, now they got to pay the price and it's high because we can't let them step on people like that. Today them Malians, pretty soon nobody have no rights, including the French," Professor May Day prophesied. In five weeks more than seventeen hundred foreigners had been expelled as a threat to public order. The security minister was quoted as saying that the criticism of his actions came from a choir of weeping women.

Tap-tap, tap tap tap . . . Tap-tap, tap tap tap . . .

"As bad as it is, some of us don't want to go back home. Here I am an artist; in Mexico, I am nothing," the sculptor said. "When I was home I felt like I was already in exile. Like nobody understood the language I was speaking . . ."

"No freedom, no rest. No freedom, no rest," the blind woman said quietly.

It became a gentle chant the room carried . . .

No freedom, no rest.

A whisper, part of our pulse . . .

No freedom, no rest.

We sat reflective for a while. The silence was broken by heavy footsteps on the stairs. Olu-Christophe said Patrick always came late. He was a pretty Eurasian bad boy, a heroin addict, who wore a black leather jacket without a shirt in eight-below or eighty-degree weather to hide the track marks that webbed his arms. Professor May Day put up with him only because he felt sorry for him, and Patrick kept pleading in his proper British boarding school accent to be taken seriously as a writer. We listened politely, but his short stories read like bad acid trips.

When Professor May Day got tired he closed his eyes and

rested his chin on his chest. Soft snoring erupted from him every few minutes, and people began to leave. I started picking up empty dishes and wine bottles. Olu-Christophe stood on the stairs smoking a cigarette, continuing his friendly argument with the Fulbright scholar. Professor May Day woke himself up with a loud snort. His eyes met mine, and he beckoned me over to sit next to him on the sofa. He put his arm around my shoulders and looked at me, his eyes darting quickly from one side of my face to the other.

"I'm gonna tell you something, and you got to promise to tell somebody. I have planted many seed but have seen few grow. I want to plant another kind of seed in you today. I want to tell you about your greatness as a black woman, and I want you to believe it, because it is true. When I first came to France, and I ain't lying, I couldn't get a soul to cuss at me till I said I was a jazz poet. French people put a crown on this head that used to be full of black wool. When I first come here I met a woman by the name of Dr. Farolyn Mae Prease. She introduced me to some of the finest cats alive to create a piece of music, a string of words, a living picture. Do you know James Baldwin? Do you know the work of Aimé Césaire? Here's eighty francs, go buy one of his books. Tomorrow morning first thing you do is go down there to Présence Africaine and buy one of his books. Do you know Countee Cullen? Le Roi Jones? I met them, seen them come, and seen many of them go on to really shine in the world. Carlene Hatcher Polite and Richard Wright lived over there by the Sorbonne, Langston too. Geniuses every one. The world ain't ready for true black genius. In every nigger is a cup of African blood from kings and queens of a divine nature, mathematicians, craftsmen, men and women of the land. I have known some sisters and brothers would scare Einstein back into East European caves with the magnificence of their minds. We are a people with a practical nature and great vision. We have built nations, discovered treasures for everyday use. Our people are a great race of people, and though the Europeans raped and plundered, we have kept inner riches. You got a cup of African blood and that mean something, means you got a responsibility to be proud of it and use your talents or suffer self-destruction."

With that advice Professor May Day patted me on my upper thigh and smiled his famous fatherly grin. I smiled too as I gently removed his hand and thanked him graciously for the message and for his hospitality.

A pretty young Asian woman appeared at the top of the stairs. She nodded toward me and Professor May Day, then put a small gift-wrapped box on the top step. She grinned widely, as if there was a secret between her and the Professor, waved, then ran back down the stairs.

"That was the daughter of one of them Sonys. I introduced her to some people. She here trying to make it on her own as a dancer. All that money and she want to live like a bohemian."

Professor May Day opened the box and passed the little origami figure to me.

"It's a paper crane. We used to make these in school," I said.

"Keep it. You the one need the luck." Professor May Day scratched his head and reached for another memory.

Olu-Christophe ran up the stairs to see what was taking me so long. I tucked a blanket around Professor May Day's shoulders and tiptoed out of the apartment and down the stairs. The talking drum was still beating in my mind. Ving was waiting for us by the fountain at the foot of boulevard St-Michel. He grinned at us, brushing his hair from his face. I felt something strong for him. I wanted to make love to the boy and the girl in him. I knew I would miss him when he was gone.

Olu-Christophe suggested we go to Montmartre. He had been paid for a house-painting job and felt rich enough to buy a bottle of wine for us to share. Walking through a small park we stumbled upon a bizarre sight. It looked like a wedding ceremony. We watched from a distance. A handsome European couple stood in a grove of trees at dusk. The woman held a white candle and was looking at the man as if he were the whole world, and he looked at her in the same way. An older man stood in front of them reading from a book. The couple exchanged rings, and we watched them kiss. Afterward, they extinguished the candle with one breath. Ving squeezed my hand and kissed me on the neck.

"Marry me," Ving said, and I laughed and pulled him away from those thoughts. Olu-Christophe's face was a hard mask.

Even though the train was nearly empty we rode in the first-class car without first-class tickets to Pigalle. I was the only one who was nervous about the conductor checking our tickets. Ving and Olu-Christophe assured me no one would be checking on a Sunday night, and no one was.

We walked up the steep narrow street that led to Sacré-Coeur and then up the hundreds of steps to the open square in front of the white stone church. Illuminated at night, it looked to me like a picture in a storybook. Dozens of people, mostly young couples, sat on the stone steps looking out over the city. Cigarette tips glowed in the darkness, along with the flames of candles stuck in the necks of wine bottles. Someone was playing a guitar and singing a Bob Dylan song off-key. We sat on a stone ledge and drank from the bottle of wine in turn. Each in our own thoughts.

We did not speak again until Ving suggested we take a walk behind the church. Artists were selling their paintings to tourists from underneath their arms, performers were singing, dancing, and eating fire. Cafés with small terraces were crowded with late-night drinkers and tourists looking for a good time. We were offered sex, drugs, and accordion lessons before we had gone once around the square. Ving stopped and bought us all chocolate crêpes. Ving licked chocolate from my hands. Walking back to the church we made music with the drum, we beat our hands and sticks against wooden fences and brick walls. We crossed the square and took one last look at the city spread out before us. We began our descent of the stairway. It was so steep I got dizzy and had to stop a few times to get my balance. When we were about a third of the way down, two policemen appeared in our path. Their uniforms looked like those in the movies—navy pants with sharp creases, starched sky blue shirts, and the cylinder-shaped hats that made them look like toy soldiers. Olu-Christophe began backing away. Ving put his arm out, pushing me behind him.

"*Arretez!*" the police shouted. They held their pistols poised at their hips.

"What is the problem, officer?" Ving spoke slowly in English. Olu-Christophe was trembling, his eyes bright with fear. He hugged his drum to his chest.

The policemen spoke harshly in French to Olu-Christophe.

"They want to see our papers," Ving repeated in a tight voice. The officers moved closer, and one of them caught Olu-Christophe by the front of his shirt.

"If you have your passport, take it out slowly," Olu-Christophe said, keeping his eyes on the tense policemen.

A flashlight was aimed on my left sock, where I had bent down to retrieve my passport. They watched carefully as I drew it out. They studied it, then shined the light in my face. Ving produced a battered U.S. passport from his back pocket. They took longer studying his. Olu-Christophe looked down at the ground and told them in French that his papers were at home. They asked him where he lived, what country he was from, and when he would be returning. They searched him roughly and finding nothing decided to take him anyway.

"He hasn't done anything," I said.

"Eden, they don't need an excuse to shoot us," Ving said between clenched teeth. "Where are you taking him?" he called to the policemen's backs.

"*A l'Afrique avec les autres singes,*" they said, and laughed.

I knew the French word for monkey. I felt as if a blow had landed squarely in my stomach. I sat on the stairs and watched them shove Olu-Christophe, still clutching his drum. His head hung low between them.

"We'd better get out of here." Ving helped me up.

"How can they just take him away? They didn't tell us where they're taking him."

"This was a bad night to be a black man without papers."

"Is there ever a good night to be black? What will they do to him?"

"Probably kick his ass and send him back to Haiti. He was asking for political asylum, but his student visa expired a long time ago. The French like their immigrants to come with degrees, money, and white skins, if at all. In Haiti, for dodging military service he'll be tried for treason. I hope like hell he's lucky."

I said a prayer he would make it out of harm's way. We asked at two police stations nearby and went every day for a week to request information about him, but we never saw Olu-Christophe again.

My situation was looking sad. The American family had left Paris, and I had found a small room which I could afford for only a week if there were no emergencies and I ate sparingly. Ving had hinted that he might be leaving Paris, and I was too proud to ask him for favors. Omar the Spaniard had been evicted from his apartment. He and his pregnant Golden Girl had moved in with Ving temporarily.

I arranged to meet Ving at a café on the boulevard Montparnasse. He was there when I arrived. As soon as I sat down he handed me a letter addressed to Irving Boncoeur. It had a Provence postmark.

"My mother is dying," he said, pushing the letter toward me.

Ving had decided to go to Provence for a few days to be with his mother before she died. She had throat cancer. He said he was still afraid of her, but he loved her and didn't know how not to go. He had not seen her in five years. She wrote him letters, but he had not responded till now.

"If she hurts you, don't stay. You're grown-up. You don't have to stay," I reminded him as I brushed his long dark curls away from his face. We both were weeping, and I was wondering if I was strong enough for the two of us.

He played his horn till his lips cracked and bled. Neither of us could disguise our pain.

I didn't want to understand what the man was asking for, because I'd have to get mad or embarassed or ashamed because I needed money so badly. My hotel had overbooked and began to charge me double the room's original price. I had no one to turn to. Delphine was still in the south, her parents hoping to keep her out of harm from terrorists' bombs. Professor May Day was attending a conference in Istanbul, and Indego was spending the winter on some Indonesian island with a new friend. I was sitting on a bench next to the pond in Parc Montsouris, trying to keep warm by rubbing my hands together and blowing on them. I reread the letter from my mother. It was written on a piece of lined stationery and made me want to get on a plane that night.

> *Dear Precious Daughter.*
> *How are you? We here are all fine. We miss you. How*
> *else can I say we wish you well and hope you find what*
> *you are looking for and come home soon? My church*
> *work keeps me busy so I don't get too lonesome with-*
> *out you and your daddy. Your aunt Victorine asks about*
> *you. You know she is no good about writing. She comes*
> *around regular these days. The weather is turning cold*
> *and I hope you are warm and have enough to eat. Here*

*is $20. I took a chance and sent cash hoping this will
reach you along with my prayers you are safe and well.
God Bless. Love, Your mother, Hermine*

I wanted to go home, but I wasn't finished yet.

A man who appeared to be in his early fifties with a thick
head of neatly combed graying hair, a small moustache, was
suddenly standing between me and the lake. His long, worn
black coat and misshapen black hat made me wonder if he was
death coming to put me out of my misery.

"You are American." It was more a statement than a question.

"Yes," I said glancing suspiciously at his hands, hoping he
didn't have a weapon.

"Please, you help me. I can give you money," he said, seeming excited by the idea.

"What for?" I stood up and moved a few steps away from him.

"You are American. You speak American. Okay?" He
seemed to think I understood, and motioned for me to follow
him. I don't know why I did, maybe because he looked harmless and he hadn't actually asked me for sex, but I still wasn't
sure what he wanted. I followed him, keeping the distance between us at least two arm's lengths. He kept looking over his
shoulder to see if I was behind him. I followed him across the
park and to the busy street on the west side. We crossed the
street and soon came to a small hotel. He started inside. I
stopped in my tracks, realizing the kind of place it was and the
kind of girl he thought I was. I started to cry.

"I won't hurt you," he said, putting his hand awkwardly on my shoulder and patting it as if it had caught on fire. "I left my books to my sister. I need you help me speak good English. I want to speak American."

Etienne worked at the Gare St. Lazare as a ticket clerk. He had always dreamed of going to America. He lived in the back of the hotel with his sister and her husband and their three small children. Until one year ago he had lived in Brittany, caring for his father before he died. His mother had died a few months earlier. He had met an American man, he said and blushed, and wanted to visit him in America.

"But my English must be good."

Once he invited me to dinner. His sister was a thick, sturdy woman with rosy cheeks. She smiled a lot but spoke no English at all. We made pantomine. The children were both still in diapers and wanted to sit on my lap and touch my skin and hair. When her husband walked in he took one look at me and walked out the door, letting it slam behind him.

Etienne and I sat in the park after that. For the next five days Etienne paid me fifty francs a day to sit next to him for one hour, listening to him read from English-language newspapers, correcting his pronunciation, and going over lessons in a book called *American English in Five Days.* At the end of the five days Etienne left to visit his American gentleman in Nebraska, and I went back to wondering if it wasn't time for me to give up and go home.

HÔTEL DES INVALIDES

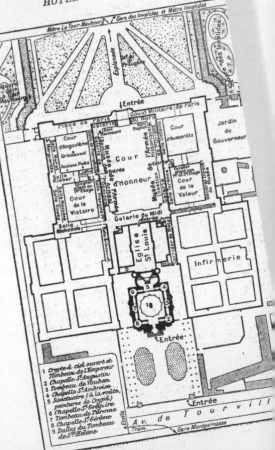

thief

AT NIGHT I STOLE COINS from a fountain near the rue St-Denis, where streetwalkers in tight midriff-baring sweaters and leather miniskirts catwalked in the shadows. Indego told me that the fountain was modeled on the Trevi Fountain, in Rome. The Parisian version was small but elaborate. It had been designed by an Italian artisan. Stony lifelike nude goddesses and half-naked nymphs frolicked under the weak flow of water spilling from the mouths of large fish. It was believed that if you threw three coins in the Trevi Fountain you would return to Rome someday. All I wanted was enough coins to stay right where I was, and I knew there would at least be enough *centimes* in the fountain for a cup of coffee and a baguette to get me through the evening.

In the same week Ving went to see his mother, Indego left again to travel without me (he told me I was selfish because of my reluctance to make love with him when I was fully awake), and my au pair family returned to the U.S. I had no job and almost couldn't afford a place to sleep. I didn't have enough money for a cup of coffee so I could sit for a few hours in a café. I still had a few days left on my *carte orange* métro card, so I took a bus from Châtelet just before sunset, getting off a few stops south of the fountain. Walking slowly along the boulevard, I looked out for policemen while I feigned fascination with the theater posters on the art nouveau kiosks and the merchandise displayed in the iron-gated shop windows. I sat on the edge of the fountain, pretending to feed the pigeons with lint and shredded pieces of gum wrappers I pulled out of the corners of my pockets. I wished I had bread to feed the scrawny gray birds cooing and gurgling around my feet, but at that moment bread was as luxurious as cake. I waited until it was dark to dip my hands into the cool water. At first all I collected were fingers full of wet trash, floating cigarette butts, and soggy half-eaten crêpes. Leaning closer to the surface I dragged my hand along the bottom as I inched my body around the edge of the fountain, looking over my shoulder to see if anyone was watching. Most of the shops on the street level were closed, and most Parisians living in the apartments above were having their evening meals. The streetwalkers were distracted by their business transactions. Most of them looked too old to be strolling along the cobblestoned streets in blond wigs and run-over high heels.

According to Indego this part of Paris was famous among World War II veterans. Soldiers had flocked to Pigalle after the liberation to drink champagne and watch lavish stage shows, or they'd gone to Strasbourg–St. Denis to spend a few hours in a hotel or enjoy a hand job on a dark side street. Now the whores of Strasbourg–St. Denis were kept busy by tourists who walked off with them in the dark. I watched them carefully. If things didn't change for me soon, I'd have to join them.

I heard a bicycle approaching behind me. In the darkness I could make out the outline of a young boy . . . or was it a girl who rode by so quickly I didn't have time to take my hand out of the water? But the cyclist passed without paying attention to me. I kept dragging the bottom. Just as I clasped another fistful of coins I heard a low hissing and saw the cyclist motioning to me from the other side of the fountain.

"*Sssssss.*" The hissing grew louder, and a finger pointed behind me. When I turned around I saw that the finger was pointing in the direction of an approaching trio of uniformed policemen known as the Peace Keepers. They were more rugged looking than the Parisian police. Young recruits from the countryside. They resembled Nazi storm troopers and wore ferocious grimaces on their baby faces. They walked three abreast, carrying their weapons slung over their shoulders with their fingers on the triggers between ready and aim. Even when I was lost I never considered asking one of the Peace Keepers for help. You didn't want to risk being hassled by them.

I snatched my hand out of the water and laid it in my lap as if I were cradling a baby. The Peace Keepers passed by, seeming to pay attention neither to me nor the streetwalkers down the block. I could now see a girl standing under the streetlight. I'd seen her before—on a noisy, ancient bicycle near the American Bookstore. The girl had stood as she did now, a little apart from the group standing around outside the shop looking at the new job and housing listings. The anemic, red-haired, gap-toothed violinist from Kansas City had dismissed her as a crazy West Indian who was not to be trusted. She didn't look crazy to me. She had probably saved me from being arrested. The girl on the bicycle gave me a wink and a smile as if we had just gotten away with something. I waved to her and hurried toward the bus stop with a handful of wet coins in my pocket. Sitting on the bus-stop bench I counted out Spanish pesetas, Russian rubles, Japanese yen, Dutch kroners, Korean won, *centime* pieces, and four French francs. I had enough worthless coins to start a collection as vast as Mason Dimple's, and I'd only had to travel to France to find them all. I soon heard the bicycle's tinkling bell roll up beside me.

"Lucienne Marie-Claire Héloise Rousseau." She extended her hand and I shook it. She had a thick, wild bush of kinky, springy curls sprouting from her head. Her smooth skin was the color of a creamy rich cappuccino, and her round open face was sprinkled with cinnamon freckles. There were dark shadows beneath her gray eyes as if she hadn't slept in days. Her body was hidden beneath layers of loose dark clothes. She straddled the old blue bicycle, her hands resting on the handlebars. She looked me up and down, as if assessing my weight and my worth. Her smile lit up the night. Large teeth so perfect her mouth could sell happiness.

"Is it so bad?" She watched me count out the coins onto the wooden bench.

"Worse," I said, separating the stacks of coins into those I could use and those I would keep as souvenirs. The hotel where I was staying had taken away my room key and was holding my bags until I could pay my bill. I hoped Ving would return soon.

"Stupid tourists sometimes throw ten-franc pieces in. I used to come here, but I was nearly killed. The street sweepers come after the tour buses leave, at three. Some of them would cut your throat for ten francs." She looked at me for a reaction to this information. I looked away from her, swept the money into my hand, and put it in my pocket.

"I'm not afraid," I lied.

"American?" She seemed impressed.

"Yes," I admitted reluctantly.

"For thirty-five francs I know where you can get the best meal in Paris." Her accent was like music.

"Can I get a bed too?" I asked.

"No rich boyfriend to spend the night with?" She laughed with her whole body.

"No money and no boyfriend, and there's nothing funny about it."

When I said this her look changed and she assessed me, this time considering my trustworthiness.

"Okay, for twenty francs I can get you a meal *and* a bed."

I wondered briefly if I was getting myself into a situation, but the choice was made for me. I could follow this strange black girl or sleep on a park bench. I gave her two ten-franc coins, and she put the money in her pocket and jingled the coins as we walked. Paris at night, on foot, is beautiful, even if you are cold, hungry, and tired. Everywhere I looked, something interesting caught my eye.

"Let's eat," she said, and I followed her down the street.

She locked her bike onto a metal stand, stretched a dark blue knit cap over her wild hair. We rode the métro two stops. That night Luce taught me how to jump the turnstile for a free ride and how to punch a used ticket for a free ride on the bus.

"If you're caught, pretend you no speak French. Be very American. Pretend you punched the wrong ticket and how stupid of you. Keep a fresh ticket at hand. Hide your money well because they will make you empty your pockets and if they find any money they will take it all and give you a ticket to appear in court. Pretend you are helpless, like a lost little girl."

I was not offended, I still felt helpless and lost. My new guide, though, was daring in ways I could only dream of. She said she could tell I was different by the way I dressed. She didn't see too many black Americans like me. Most were well dressed and rich or students on holiday, academics on grants or white-collar workers for multinational corporations.

"It's hard to meet black women. The atmosphere is very cold. I wanted to approach you, but I was afraid the others had poisoned you against me. The guy with the red hair I saw you with, the zombie, he tried to grab my breasts and I ran over him with my bicycle."

"He said you were crazy and couldn't be trusted."

"He told the others I stole from him, but I didn't really. I only took what belonged to me."

The restaurant was in a part of the city where I'd never been. It was large and opened onto the boulevard for sidewalk service. Through the window we could see several waiters smoking at the bar, telling jokes. The diners were mostly tourists dressed casually, but the prices on the menu posted in the front window were expensive. As we entered the restaurant I watched Luce steal a handful of spoons and a tiny oyster fork from a service table.

"What are you going to do with all those spoons?" I whispered as we sat at a table near the door.

"Make music," she said clapping two spoons together in the palm of her hand under the table, then slipping them into a pocket hidden in the wide sleeve of her coat meant for just such opportunities.

Our waiter was young and wore his hair slicked back and high on his head like a Fifties biker. His black jacket and pants were shiny with age and the once-white apron at his waist was dirty. He did not even try to speak to us in French, which I could tell irritated Luce, who smiled at him and then made a sour face to me. He thought we were tourists. It was hilarious to hear her speak with an American accent. She tried to mimic me, but it came out sounding like American television actors trying to talk Southern. Our waiter attempted to impress us in English with his mouth-watering descriptions of the *specialités* of the house.

Luce ordered a feast for us. She started with a tray of oysters on the half shell and a chilled silver plate with small pale green boats of endive lettuce leaves arranged in a star pattern with dabs of blue cheese, walnuts, and freshly chopped herbs nestled in each leaf. I was dazzled and made light-headed by the beautiful displays and nearly fainting with hunger, not having eaten since morning. Luce dressed each oyster with a *squirt* of lemon and swallowed it with relish. I ate the lettuce boats, barely tasting the cheese or chewing the nuts. We did not speak through most of the meal. Occasionally Lucienne would stab at something on my plate and chew on it thoughtfully, and her facial expression would show her pleasure. My next course was a perfectly roasted cornish hen the size of a small fist that sat in a pool of creamy lemon-flavored gravy garnished with sprigs of thyme and surrounded by soft, sweet, golden roasted potatoes and a few blanched green beans. Luce was presented with a fish-shaped plate of broiled filet of sole in a white butter sauce with a small hill of crispy golden fried potato balls and a tiny bouquet of overcooked cauliflower. We both ate quickly, washing every other bite down with a swallow or two of a thick Burgundy. I started to feel a little nauseous, the food was so rich. Before we walked in the door I suspected that Luce didn't have enough to pay for the meal. I knew it was a sin, but I did it anyway and prayed for forgiveness to the god of hunger. I wondered if Luce had a bug in a jar or long dark hairs to stir into what was left of the sauce. At that point I didn't care, I was satisfied and certain I could endure hours of dishwashing if necessary, I just didn't want to find out what the inside of a French jail looked like.

"I always drink red wine no matter what I'm eating because I prefer the taste. It's strong, this wine. We will sleep well tonight," Luce said, raising her glass.

"Here's to sweet dreams." I raised my glass too and looked around nervously for our waiter.

We ended our meal with double espressos and shared a white chocolate mousse cake encircled by a moat of raspberry sauce. When the waiter left the bill, Luce winked at him and made a joke with him in French.

"Your French is perfect," he said, collecting our plates. When he walked away from our table, Luce took out the twenty francs I had given her and left it on the table along with another thirty-five, even though the bill was over three hundred francs. Luce had perfect timing. She knew how to draw out the meal and waited until our waiter was serving a table on the far side of the room with his back to us before she beckoned to me to leave. We walked out of the restaurant slowly; because we were close to the door we didn't have far to go. In a few steps we were on the sidewalk and blending into a thick crowd of tourists erupting from a bus. We turned down a dark street at the first corner we came to. We ran until we felt safe, and after a few blocks we saw a métro station and slid down the handrail. Our luck was good, a train was waiting for us. We got off the train a few stops later and picked up Luce's bike.

"That was the best meal I've ever had," I said.

"It wasn't bad. Pity we can't go there again." She nodded to an old woman who had been staring at us. The woman dropped her eyes and gripped her purse closer to her body.

I didn't know where we were going or what would happen next, but I followed her as she rolled her bike between us the length of Paris in the dark. I followed the sound of her voice. She told me her life story, and I told her mine. We walked and talked for what seemed like hours, as if we'd known each other all our lives.

She was born in Barbados. She had a younger sister. Her father was a lab technician at a local hospital and her mother was a French nurse. The marriage did not last; her mother abandoned the family, and her father fell apart. He moved the family to London, where he became a taxi driver and left the girls to a string of neighborhood women who baby-sat them.

When they were older they lived on the streets of London and came home only to change their clothes.

"Have you tried to find your mother?"

"No." She looked away from me. "That's a lie. I found her family, but they wouldn't tell me where she was. I don't care about her anymore. She's not important to me." Luce was trying to convince me of this. I could hear the soldier in her voice, cold and hard. I changed the subject.

"Have you met Indego?" I asked her.

"That queer-looking guy who lays about at the American Bookstore? I met him, but I wasn't his type."

Then it was my turn to become quiet.

"What do you like to read?" I finally asked her.

"Whatever is easy to pinch."

"Do you like Baldwin? He wrote . . ."

"I know who he is. I saw him on the telly one time, cutting some white guy to ribbons about how the Americans had treated black Vietnam War vets. I read *Giovanni's Room* a long time ago. Baldwin's a good writer but depressing as hell. I don't ever want to love like that."

"Maybe that was the point," I said.

"What?"

"To take risks for love, not to be afraid of it."

"I'm through with all that. I want to forget about love. We start by going shopping tomorrow. There's a good bookstore in Montmartre that sells English books." I was afraid of the kind of shopping we would do without money.

Lucienne explained to me that a friend had given her the key to his parents' apartment. They were Americans who used the

apartment only in late spring and summer. We finally reached
an elegant old building on a quiet street in the west of Paris, near
the Bois de Boulogne. We passed the darkened windows of the
concierge's apartment at the gated entrance to the building on
the ground floor. The building faced the river. Its white stone
façade was decorated with delicate wrought-iron balconies.
Luce punched in the code and we entered the dark entrance
hall. She found the light, and the slick black marble floor beneath us shone like black pearls. She used a key from a chain
around her neck to open the mailbox. She pulled out a small
packet of letters, among them a brown envelope she sniffed ex-
citedly. She motioned for me to be quiet as she unlocked the
glass door and entered the mirrored foyer. We stepped lightly
on the thick dark green carpet. We squeezed into the blond
wood–paneled elevator with her bike and got off on the third
floor. We walked to the end of a long white hall hung with small
crystal chandeliers, gilded wall sconces, and gold-framed mir-
rors. We came to huge wooden double doors. I half expected
Madame Fabre's maid to open the door. I couldn't believe my
luck. Luce unlocked the door, and I followed her into the apartment. There were more chandeliers, and the entire entrance was
mirrored, so it felt as if we had stepped into a circus fun house.
Sparkles threw the light over us like a shower of golden coins.
The living room was as big as a ballroom, with the mother of all
chandeliers glittering in its center. The molding around the ceiling had intricately carved garlands of leaves and flowers. The
walls were a cool gray and on them hung large, ugly abstract
paintings. The floors were glossy inlaid wooden parquet. The
windows facing the river were at least eight feet tall and shuttered

from the outside. Dark gray velvet curtains hung to the floor like still water. The living room was sparsely furnished with uncomfortable-looking modern black-leather-and-stainless-steel furniture, some of it covered by pale linen sheets. Luce named a Swedish designer we figured must've been a sadist. The long hallway that led from the foyer to the kitchen was a gallery of black-and-white Cartier-Bresson photographs.

I was almost blinded when Luce flipped the lightswitch as we entered the white-on-white kitchen outfitted with brushed stainless steel appliances.

"Are you sure it's okay for us to be here?"

"Robert is a pal. He gave me the key. No problem."

I was feeling desperate enough to believe her. I'd stay for a few days, just until Ving returned.

The stainless steel island in the center of the room looked like an operating table. Luce sat on it and opened the small brown envelope. She peeled the plastic wrap from a small lump of a black waxy sweet-smelling substance. She told me it was hashish, sent to her by a friend in Morocco. She pulled out a pack of unfiltered cigarettes and took one out. With a toothpick she unpacked some of the tobacco at one end and mixed it with a small pinch of the hashish, then replaced it in the cigarette, twisting the tip with her long fingers. She lit the cigarette and inhaled deeply. She closed her eyes and held the smoke in her lungs for a long time, then passed the cigarette to me. It smelled like burning leaves. The third time I inhaled, I felt my lungs expand like balloons. The sound of my breath was as loud as the wind at the ocean. We finished the joint in silence, walking through the rooms. I felt warm and slow, as if I were moving through invisible clouds.

The bedroom was the smallest room, white on white. A huge circular bed sat on a raised platform in the center of the room. The chairs and nightstands nearly blended in with the walls. I followed Luce into the bathroom, which was also white with stainless steel fixtures. There were hundreds of tiny silver lightbulbs set in the ceiling. The wall above the double sinks was a sheet of beveled mirrored doors. There were two toilets and a bidet. The tub was long and deep. I saw myself in the mirror. I looked like hell. My face was thinner than I remembered, and my clothes were wrinkled and hung from my body. I looked tired, but I felt invigorated.

I went back into the bedroom, and Luce and I sat down on the bed. It felt soft, and I leaned back as if sinking into water. I wanted to lie there forever. My head was spinning, so I closed my eyes. When I opened them a few seconds or a few minutes later, brilliant jewel like colors were radiating from the ceiling and walls.

fuchsia . . . turquoise . . . lapis . . . ruby . . . amber . . . aqua . . . saffron . . . emerald . . .

Then the walls opened up, and thousands of butterflies swarmed into the room, fluttering on my eyelids and lighting in my hair. I heard the sound of the colors. I had brilliant thoughts, knew things about about the world clearly, then promptly forgot them. My head felt so light I thought the butterflies had lifted me off the bed. I floated, semiconscious, into the luminous atmosphere.

When Luce nudged me, I fell from a great height back into my body and the butterflies disappeared, but the volume was still turned up and colors were brighter. She poured us each a large snifter of brandy. Luce started dancing around the room, taking off her clothes as she moved to invisible music. Her body was abundant with curves. I marveled at the creamy texture of her skin. When she was down to her plain white cotton panties and bra she composed, conducted, and performed the silver-spoon orchestra. She played well, slapping the spoons against her bare thighs, on the soles of her feet and her soft, vibrant belly. I stripped to my underwear too. We laughed, danced, chased each other around the rooms and made music until the neighbors started banging on the wall. Exhausted, we fell asleep on the big white bed.

We were both getting over a loss. Lucienne had a boyfriend, a sailor who kept her waiting in the rain for seven hours.

The two of us felt stranded, but we were plotting our own rescue. We would sail away to Bali, fly a plane to Cape Verde. Climb mountains and sleep next to waterfalls. We would be free. I would write books, and she would paint pictures and make art from objects she found near the sea. We tried to make each other forget how much we missed having someone to love, and started to love each other.

Our days were spent sleeping until late morning. We each took a bath in the long steel tub, then had coffee and a piece of fruit.

Luce loved oranges. Watching her peel them was a small drama. She would hold the orange in her left hand, then push her right thumb into the crown of the fruit. She would slowly curl the flesh into a spiral as if she were meditating. She kept it close to her face breathing in the smell deeply as if she were having an orgasm. Blood oranges, tangerines, sauterines, tangelos, and clementines. She separated the sections and took each piece into her mouth, chewing slowly with her eyes closed as juice trickled down her chin.

It was Luce who taught me to take what I needed to get by until all possibilities were exhausted. She said thieving or pinching was better than selling your body, but if it came to that she taught me how to get by.

how to be a whore (if all else fails)

1. *Be an illusionist.* Take as much as you can from a date. Let him think it's his idea to buy you a meal or a new pair of shoes. Encourage him to talk about his problems for as long as you can. He may forget his need for sex.

2. *Encourage your date to drink.* Dates are easier to handle when they are drunk, and drinking, as all women know, can kill performance. If he can still walk, take him to the hotel just off the rue de Rivoli, the one with the blue door. They rent rooms by the hour, and the old woman on the desk looks out for the girls, so make sure to tip her at least twenty francs.

3. *Make sure your date takes a bath, even if you have to give him one yourself.* That way you can see if he has sores on his private parts, and if you are clever with a bit of soap you can get a small refund on the room deposit and go home early.

4. *Take off as little clothing as possible.* Try to get your date to come before he gets inside you. You don't want to worry about accidents. Life is hard enough for one.

5. *Bait your hook for big fish or else you will end up like the whores in Strasbourg–St. Denis who live on sardines and the kindness of strangers.*

6. *If your date is a woman, be careful—she will either try to save you from the streets or turn you out and pimp you like a man.* If anyone tries to save you and you want to be saved make sure he or she is rich, life is hard enough for one.

"If you want to catch a fish you've got to think like one, but I'm not telling you all of my secrets," Luce said as the hashish took hold of her thinking. I was already flying high above the city on gossamer wings.

Luce was no ordinary thief; she had style and technique. She stole mostly to survive, but sometimes she stole for fun. Fragrant Bluemountain coffee from Jamaica, sharp manchego cheese from Spain, crisp English water crackers, dry champagne, smooth merlot from Provence, and once, red caviar. Only once, because after a taste of the oily fish eggs she gagged and spit on the floor. I became her partner in crime. I was too nervous to actually take anything. My job was to distract the shopkeeper (mostly men, women were much more observant and suspicious of us) while Luce walked up and down the aisles, filling the deep inside pockets of her coat with as much as she could carry. Sometimes I would buy a piece of fruit or a carton of milk to keep the shopkeeper's attention, counting out small coins slowly onto the counter, apologizing in my broken French. I was charming, so we never got caught.

"You don't need a lot of money to live in Paris. You don't

need money or a man to get by, all it takes is courage," Luce said. She had plenty of that.

"You looked lost," she said, remembering. "I passed you on my bike and thought how much you looked like my sister."

"Where is she?"

"I don't know. She disappeared a long time ago."

"We can be sisters," I said, and she nodded and kissed me on the side of my face and took my hand in hers. I knew she was trying to resist being sentimental. She didn't want to wake up and find me gone like everyone else.

Then bombs began to bloom like mushroom clouds. November 1, a bomb was set off at the state-owned Minerva Airlines to protest the government deportation of the 101 Malians. November 3, there was an explosion in the headquarters of the government immigration office. No one was hurt. November 11, three bombs were set off in French companies to protest South African president Botha's visit to Paris. There were anti-apartheid protests against French military support of South Africa. Luce said that when she first arrived in Paris she met a white South African who had asked her to deliver letters for him. She told him she was not a revolutionary. She said she wanted to support the brothers and sisters in South Africa, but the French shoot to kill, and although she didn't mind jail she wasn't ready to die.

One morning in the métro station at Raspail the stairs were littered with flyers about the motives and objectives of Action Direct, a French terrorist group. The international news kiosk displayed headlines about the assassination of George Besse. It was rumored that the assassins got away on a motorbike, dressed like French whores. Action Direct claimed responsibility. My bag and passport were checked twice that day. Everyone was suspicious that anyone could have a bomb in her backpack.

One night a huge winter storm blew in from the north. I woke up cold, and my mouth was dry and tasted foul. I could see my breath. Small white clouds hung in the air. There was no heat. Luce was still passed out. I ran around the rooms putting on more clothes and searched the apartment until I found the linen closet and dragged a pile of flannel sheets and two down comforters into the bedroom. I crawled back under the covers with Luce, who was shivering. The sheets were wet with her sweat.

"Can I do something for you?" I was worried. She had a fever.

"Tell me a story," she said. Her eyes were closed, and she sounded as if her mouth was filled with cotton. The only form of literature I'd seen in the apartment was interior decorating, fashion, and cooking magazines.

"What kind of story?" I held her hand under the covers.

"Tell me a blue story."

I knew she didn't mean a sad story, so I began as I had with my dolls so long ago.

"Once upon a time, in a little blue house on the edge of a deep blue sea, lived a little girl who picked roses from the branches of blue trees . . ." I kept the story going even after she'd fallen asleep.

The next morning I forced her to go see Stephano, the Greek medical student she used to date. He told her she probably had pneumonia and prescribed antibiotics.

"I think you should go home. My offer is still good. A one-way ticket. You should go back." Stephano sounded as if he'd said this to her a thousand times, and still she waved him away. Sweat dampened her sallow face. We took a taxi, courtesy of Stephano, back to the apartment.

A few nights later, when they found us, we had spent the evening making a sculpture. We took turns piling pieces of furniture in the center of the room, balancing objects for our amusement and trying to keep warm. The nights were getting colder, and Lucienne's cough wouldn't go away.

When they entered the apartment I was dancing with a piece of raspberry cake. We had smoked the last of the hashish earlier in the day and were exhausted and hungry. It was too cold to go outside, and Luce was getting weaker, so we ate the last of the raspberry cake she had stolen from a bakery close to the house. We heard a man and a woman laughing in the dark. I thought it was me and Ving, that my missing him had conjured him up. The laughter stopped abruptly when the man entered the bedroom and saw me dancing with the piece of cake. Luce was asleep with silver spoons sticking out of her hair. They were both wearing long fur coats. The woman screamed a little scream and covered her mouth.

"What are you doing here?" the man shouted in perfect American English. "Who are you?"

"I am Countess Mea Culpa, and may I present the Duchess . . ." Luce drawled sleepily.

"Get the hell out of here before I call the police." He grabbed at the covers on the bed, but Luce held on tight. She pulled herself up and opened her eyes. I sobered quickly and looked around for a large blunt object with which to protect us if necessary.

"I remember you," he said, dropping the covers as if they were hot. "You were here with my stepson Robert in the spring . . ."

"Excellent memory, sir. I had lunch with you and your wife. She was very nice to me." The young woman in the fur coat moved back into the doorway. "Robert said I could stay in the apartment if I needed a place to stay. It was cold and we had nowhere else to go."

"He had no right to do that. You can't stay here." The man didn't want to hear about our troubles.

"Is your wife in Paris? I'm sure she'd help us."

The young woman in the fur coat began whispering to the man in French and trying to pull him out of the room. I noticed that she was carrying a large shopping bag from Hermès and on her feet were a pair of black patent leather shoes with four-inch heels. I found my socks and started putting on my shoes.

The man pulled out his wallet and tossed a handful of large franc notes onto the bed.

"I want you out of here now. And don't come back," he threatened. "Or next time I will call the police."

We gathered our few things together, scooped up the money off the bed, and stepped out into the cold Paris night. A few snowflakes were starting to fall. Luce coughed constantly as we rolled her bike to the rundown little hotel near Beaubourg off the rue de Rivoli. We got a small room with a double bed and bath down the hall, and paid for two nights in advance. There were clean sheets on the bed, but the room smelled of sex and cigarettes. We slept close together to keep warm. It felt like sleeping in a refrigerator. I sang us a blues song, and we fell asleep in each other's arms.

❧

The next day Luce wanted to go to the Turkish baths. She wanted to float in perfumed pools of liquid glass. Luce insisted we share one last extravagance. She had decided to go home. I was both excited by the exotic idea of a public bath and worried about the little bit of money we had left, but Lucienne's powers of persuasion were strong.

She'd persuaded me the week before to accompany her to a house she'd cleaned for pay. When we arrived the woman who had hired Luce wasn't home, and the baby-sitter, a timid, pig-tailed teenager, hadn't wanted to let us in, but Lucienne pushed past her and walked through the house as if she paid rent there. Out of sight of the baby-sitter, Luce swept a credit-card receipt and several sheets of embossed stationery into the bike bag slung across her chest. We sat at the kitchen table in an uncomfortable silence. The clock on the wall ticked, the baby cried, and the re-frigerator hummed like a large heart beating too fast. I was used to Luce's faraway looks and quiet conversation. She was frus-trated, angry, and I could tell she was about to do something for which she'd have no explanation later. Sure enough, after about an hour Luce stood up and walked over to the kitchen window and looked out at the one-lane lap pool in the backyard. For the third time the baby-sitter came into the kitchen and threat-ened to call the police. To Luce she was a faraway noise. I fol-lowed Luce out the back door and into the small, neatly manicured yard surrounded by a thick, square hedge. She took off her coat and handed it to me along with her socks and shoes. She stood on the edge of the pool and pulled a battered silver flask from a pocket in her dress and drank long and deep before she let gravity pull her body into the freezing, leaf-littered water. She swam back and forth until the woman who owned the house and had hired her to clean appeared in the back doorway looking scared. Luce had decided she deserved a day's pay, although the only things she had done were drink the woman's fifty-year-old scotch and load the dishwasher and fill her pockets with birdseed for the scrawny pigeons in the park near where we were living. The woman's hands were trembling when she handed Luce the envelope with the money in it. Luce counted the money twice, then handed me the envelope.

"Don't come here again." The woman backed away from us and went inside the house, slamming the door behind her. I could see her and the baby-sitter watching us out the window.

Wet and shivering, Luce wrapped herself in her coat and pulled on her socks and shoes. It started to rain; cold, fat drops hard as hail pelted us.

"I need a drink," she said, planting her feet far apart. With one hand on her hip, she took another pull from the silver flask. We laughed and ran until we found cover in an open doorway. It stopped raining after a while, but it grew colder and the sky turned dark.

"I've got to pee," Luce said. She stepped off the sidewalk between two parked cars, squatted down, pulled her underwear aside.

Her cough started the night after she spent the entire contents of the envelope on drinks for everyone in the bar we ended up in Montparnasse. Luce made a lot of friends that night, but they all were gone or passed out by morning. By the second day she had a fever. She slept restlessly, sweating through the sheets each night.

The sad, bumpy bus ride to the baths took us through the center of Paris, past narrow streets, crowded byways, antique shops, and art galleries. I had to make a decision too. I still didn't have a job, and that meant we would have to leave the hotel soon. We had barely enough money to last a week, even with our last sticky-fingered shopping spree. Lucienne persuaded me that our impoverished state was only temporary. She seemed so sure.

Lucienne pulled the cord, silently signaling the driver that we wanted to get off. The bus stopped near the Gare D'Austerlitz, the mammoth old train station. It was full of travelers steadily moving through the terminal. We walked past a café where several rude little boys were having a spitting contest and old men wearing black berets played *boules* in the dirt. The old men smiled at us. Their arched backs looked youthful as they pitched and tossed. The silver balls gleamed in the sunlight.

We walked through the gates of the Jardin des Plantes, the perfectly manicured, mathematically exact garden, all angles and straight lines. Stunning, color-coordinated flowers grew in soldierly rows. We walked slowly through the garden until we came to another set of gates. Without warning, Lucienne grabbed hold of the bars. Her body shook with measured tremors. Her breathing was hollow and rattled. Her body was rigid. She pulled the steel bars toward her with all her strength as if she were trying to rip them from the pavement. I placed a hand on her shoulder, then made circles with my palm along her spine, gently calling her name. Lucienne became still as sud-

denly as she had started. She leaned her head against my shoulder, her body sagged into mine until she began to breathe nor-
mally. A few moments later she raised her head, a drained,
weak expression on her haggard face.

"My insides are burning." Lucienne stepped away from the
fence and we linked arms. She made a move as if to march.

"Let us praise the body temple. Let us be cleansed." There
was hope in her hoarse voice.

"You've been to this *Hammam* before?" I asked as we passed
the entrance to the *mosquée*.

"No, not here. The first time, my sister and I went together
in Tunis. I had never seen so many naked women together, so
at ease. In Barbados sometimes we bathed in the river after
dark. My back was always turned to the others. I was very shy.
I was ignorant of my body. I had a big fear of being exposed."
Her hands opened outward as if offering me a gift.

"At home I would bathe in a white cotton dress because the
old Irish woman who baby-sat my sister and me taught us that
it was a sin to touch our bodies too directly. When I found out
how good it felt to touch myself I would lock myself in the bathroom for hours using a big bar of white soap to lather my chest
and between my legs under the dress until the water was cold."

We laughed at our old selves and held hands as we ran across
the street. I wished she were my sister, the strong one, the pro-
tector, except now she needed me.

A veiled woman and her teenaged daughter entered the
Hammam before us, hand in hand. In the courtyard, a secret
garden, lush, moist, and timeless, opened to us. Weathered
turquoise tiles covered the walkway. Once-white tiles deco-

rated with cinnamon, black, and green designs snaked along the lower walls and entryways. A green-tiled roof. A fountain, its base an eight-pointed star, stood at the center of the verdant garden. Slender silver-leafed olive trees grew silently in the rich dark earth. We entered a low archway, then passed through heavy wooden doors. Heat assaulted us. Our lungs were unprepared for the blast of stifling hot air. A dark young woman with oily black hair and mandalas tattooed on her forehead and chin drew back the heavy black curtains covering the entrance. Behind an elevated desk a weathered old Arab woman wearing a worn black uniform collected our admission fee. There were faded henna designs on the back of her wrinkled hands. Her hair hung down her back in a long neat braid. She smiled at us, revealing several gold teeth. She gave us a small flat square of wood with the number seven on it. She put the basket with our valuables in it behind the counter.

What I saw was a secret garden of naked women. A modern harem. The light was dim in the inner courtyard. On either side of a bubbling marble fountain shaped like a large seashell, beneath a ceiling of windows with frosted panes, were long raised platforms veiled by sheer curtains. Thick green vinyl mats lined the upper platform areas in a neat horizontal row, about a dozen on each side. Naked and half-naked women reclined on the individual mats, some sleeping in pairs, their mats pushed together, others combing and oiling each other's hair, massaging and lotioning moist flesh. The air was hot and damp. A few women lay holding hands, whispering, their eyes on the newcomers.

I was shy and curiously excited all at once. My worries began to drift away. My focus shifted. After disrobing and laying our clothes on two free mats we opened the heavy door just beyond the two resting areas. Air even warmer and heavier enveloped us. Towels in hand we passed through the fluorescent-lit shower room, where a few women were washing under a row of shower heads the size of dinner plates. A toothless woman in her fifties wearing a modest dark blue bathing suit and black rubber sandals appeared to be using a rough black cloth to scrub a layer of skin from the back of another woman who lay on a marble slab that jutted out from the wall. There was the sound of water running, steam hissing, and soap lathering, the harmonic grunts of the woman scrubbing and her client. The women whispered. We were in a sacred place. In the absence of men these women made themselves vulnerable to one another. The woman with the veil and her daughter were ahead of us, naked now, still hand in hand. They disappeared through distant doors.

We moved through the steam into the next chamber of the labyrinth, which was empty and even hotter. The walls and floor were pale gray-veined marble. Open cubicles were on either side of us. We sat on the floor of one of the cubicles, folding our towels under our bottoms, trying to adjust to the heat. Sweat began to drip from our bodies. Luce lay down and closed her eyes.

"*Ça va?*" Luce asked.

"*Ça va,*" I answered weakly.

I wiped sweat from above her eyes.

Acutely aware of my sweating body, freed of the restrictions of clothes, I began to be aware of a desire within myself. A desire I had been supressing for weeks. It scared me to think that it was possible I was in love with a woman. When Luce was sick and I thought I'd lose her I realized that she'd become more than a friend. We depended on each other. I could see that loving her could consume me. I could not see us living a life together without end. But I couldn't get her out of my thoughts. I ran my hands across my belly and let images float behind my closed eyelids. Hands on my salty face, neck, breasts, inner thighs.

"Are you afraid of *SIDA?*" Luce disturbed my thoughts.

"AIDS? What makes you think about that? The Action Direct bombs are scarier." Luce twisted her body from one uncomfortable position to another. "For a woman to be with another woman seems to be the safest choice."

"Have you ever been with a woman?"

"Of course," Luce answered without hesitation. "I have slept with many men as well. But love has not always been the motive. With men, sex is so quick and easy. I prefer women as lovers, but men offer more material things. If you are lucky a man can give you a house and beautiful children to hold, but only a woman can truly love another woman." Lucienne sounded so certain. She reached over and squeezed my hand. I squeezed back.

"Maybe I can love you if you want? You have given me so much. You saved me," she whispered. There were tears in her eyes.

"You don't owe me anything." I felt a lump in my throat. I wished I could be sure that making love wouldn't change us, but I knew well the way Luce used sex to pay her debts. I wanted to touch her, but I didn't want sex to jeopardize our friendship. "You're leaving tomorrow. Don't break my heart too."

"You make me want to keep a part of you with me always." Lucienne touched my face with her fingers.

When I didn't move or speak she said, "Come, let's get closer to the fire." She pulled me to my feet.

We heard laughter as we passed through the door at the far end of the cubicle room, where we discovered the heart of the inferno. It was the hottest room in the belly of the baths. Swirls of steam surrounded a dozen or so naked women of varying ages and shapes. The heat made everyone's skin flush. A few of the women stared at us openly. We heard loud whispers in German and Italian. The veiled woman and her daughter were in a corner of the room. The mother braided the daughter's hair, then the daughter clipped her mother's toenails. They changed positions, then took turns scrubbing each other's bodies, quietly, reverently. After a while Luce took my hand and led me back into the shower room.

"I was close to fainting," Luce whispered.

We lathered under the cool, stinging water of the shower, then toweled dry, returning to the inner courtyard, where we lay side by side on the foam mats. I began to dream.

There are five women sitting around a large fire, dressed in tropical bird feathers. "Where am I?" I ask repeatedly, trying to cover my nakedness with my hands. The women answer me, but I can't understand them. After a while I realize that no one here speaks my language.

When I woke up, Luce's arm was thrown over my bare waist, and she had snuggled close to me in her sleep. We lay naked underneath a thin white sheet damp from the humidity.

Her breath on my back was cool and steady. The smell of mint, the sound of running water, the taste of salt on my lips, the steady gaze of women's eyes caressing each other. I was uncomfortable not only because of the heat but also because of the nearness of another woman's body. No one seemed to notice us. After my childhood games with Rosaleen were finished, I had never thought of kissing another woman, but Luce was so close, her skin so soft. I breathed as she breathed. I wanted to mold my flesh into hers, sink and dive beneath the surface of her skin and swim and swim and swim. She offered her body to me, and we touched. When Luce stroked my hair I felt loved. Her invisible kisses were cool, minty. I touched her in places I couldn't see. Liquid, fragrant blooms, opening.

The veiled woman and her daughter were applying kohl to their eyes, looking in a small gold compact. They began to put on their veils carefully. Watching them through half-open eyes I felt like a voyeur. I closed my eyes and fell back to sleep.

"It's time to go. Wake up," Luce whispered hoarsely.

My heart sank because it was also time to say good-bye. I didn't know how I could let her go. I tried to think of a way we could stay together, but we had run out of luck. I had so little to offer her. I was still dreaming. I didn't believe then that love alone could save us. I thought of Dr. Bernard and Mason Dimple, of Giovanni and David, and wondered if I was missing an opportunity or letting go too soon.

We showered again without looking at each other and dressed in our street clothes, tipping the attendant on our way out. Inside the Turkish café to the right of the garden, several Muslim men in traditional clothing and a few foreigners sat at tables with huge round brass trays for tops. Turkish rugs hung on the wall and covered the floor. Men drank syrupy tea and ate honeyed sweets. Luce and I sat by a window quietly, in our own thoughts, drinking our tea from tiny, colorful glasses, watching the other patrons. We both stole glances at the women we had moments before seen naked. My eyes were drawn to an Arab woman whose lush brown body I had seen in the showers. She wore a tiger-print fez over her dark hair, which she had pulled back into a French braid. Her plump face was made-up, and though her sculpted features were beautiful, her eyes were sad. She wore a sheer black blouse with pockets covering her pendulous, otherwise bare breasts, tight black leather pants, and jewel-studded leather sandals on her tiny pedicured feet. Her movements were sensual. She sat alone by a window, smoking a thin clove cigarette. My lips burned for a taste of the sweet smoke. After a while the woman went outside and got into the back of a chauffeured white Mercedes and was driven away. I tried to think of ways to heal Luce, to seduce her, to make her stay.

A regal African woman with a baby wrapped on her back walked past our window like a bored queen. She wore a bright orange robe and matching *gelee* on her head, dusty sandals. Her arms were weighted with gold jewelry. She carried a large woven basket. I thought for a moment I was in Africa. Her beauty radiated from her high forehead, wide round eyes, and high cheeks; her nose and lips shone. I wondered if there was still milk in her breasts under the orange robe. I wanted Lucienne to stay, but I kept myself busy seducing other women in my mind because it was safe.

"When I am well, when I see you again, I am going to love you completely." Luce kissed my mouth, lingered, burning herself into me.

I hoped someday she would forgive me for letting her go.

> They stare at us
> on the Paris métro
> two happy black women
> together
> really together
> our arms linked in solidarity.
> There is so much more than they see.
> Our joy is loud.
> We laugh and dance
> down the aisles,
> even though our hands have worn holes in our pockets
> searching for coins that aren't there.
> She is my water
> and also my thirst.
> We are not just friends,
> we are sisters,
> African kin.
> There is so much more than they see.

II. CHAMPS ÉLYSÉES. LOUVRE.

15

METRO

271340

les musées

COLLECTION PERMANENTE
ENTRÉE
Plein Tarif A

artist's model II: vence

VING WAS THINNER when he came back from visiting his mother. He looked as if he had seen a ghost. He found me in front of the American Bookstore, looking for work. I was happy to see him. I asked about his mother, but he wouldn't talk about his visit with her except to say that he had a pocketful of money and he wanted to spend some of it on me. We quickly fell into a routine of easing our pain in each other's company. He insisted I stay with him at his place for a while. Omar the Spaniard and his Golden Girl had moved into a new apartment. I was reluctant to take his offer, not wanting to become too dependent on him. There was nothing free about being a kept woman. He told me not to worry about taking advantage of his generosity, there was a favor he wanted to ask of me, a big one. He said he had plans for me, plans for us.

The purple satin dress was too short and too tight, but the glass of brandy was strong enough to make me fearless about standing up on a stage the size of a kitchen table and singing to a roomful of people. Ving adjusted the thin straps on my borrowed dress and kneeled down to tighten the clasps on the silver high heels he'd found under a bench in the dilapidated dressing room of his friend Guillermo's bar. Ving kissed the inside of my wrist. His hair brushed against my arm. With his hair down he looked like a girl, and at first it felt strange, but after a while I liked the idea. He seemed to me a new kind of sex, neither man nor woman. He became aroused, making me up like a porcelain doll, dressing me in exotic costumes he found at the flea market, silk saris and brocade Chinese robes, earth-colored African mud cloth, and huge peacock feather fans and nothing else at all. When we made love I closed my eyes and Luce was kissing my shoulder, Ving was touching my lips. Luce's hand on my breasts, Ving's hair brushing against my navel.

In the borrowed dress I wore the night I sang the blues, I looked like Billie Holiday, Ving thought. He'd even bought a gardenia to put behind my ear. It was brown at the edges, but he said it wouldn't matter in the dim light. Omar the Spaniard was desperate. His girlfriend, who was seven and a half months pregnant, had attempted to do a split during their show, and halfway to the floor her water broke. The second Golden Girl was so startled she passed out, breaking her index finger in the fall. A few hours later Omar's girlfriend gave birth to a girl she named James Brown Serafino. Omar begged me in Spanish, French, English, and grammar school Latin to sing for one week in the club. It would give him time to find new Golden Girls and rehearse them. He assured me Guillermo loved blues music, and Ving had told him I used to sing. What I didn't know was that sometimes girls performed stripteases on the stage between acts and some of the customers were expecting that.

"The French love African American music. Billie Holiday is very big here. Sing her songs and I will name my next child after you."

"Don't do your children any more favors." I was secretly glad for the chance to perform. Guillermo didn't actually care whether I sang. He just wanted me to entertain the crowd. I quickly drank the rest of the brandy Ving gave me for courage and moved toward the stage.

This was not the first time I sang the blues. My secular singing was at first a secret. My mother took me to choir practice and from the time I was very small I would sing along. When I was only four she made me join the youth choir, where I sang solos during holiday services. After Aunt Victorine got hold of me, every time I tried to sing in church it came out sounding like the blues. That's how Mama found out I had a blossoming career in juke joints. In college I auditioned to sing in a club. The manager of the bar said I had too much religion. I couldn't win for losing.

"You sound like Aretha when she was holy. We need something you can dance to, make people sweat, make them want to drink a lot." I took the comparison to Aretha as a compliment, but I did not get the job.

Ving had his own sound, and he played it for me. It was soulful and sad, a new kind of blues, he said. He was in demand as a musician because he was like a sea sponge when he played with other bands. His ear was like a tape recorder, he could play back any sound he heard. Some patrons wondered out loud if Ving had any African blood in him. When Ving played standards with a French quartet near Beaubourg he was paid in cash at the end of the evening. With the Latins he played salsa with a Spanish accent. The Latins paid him weeks late but always made up for it by partying until dawn after their gigs and giving him free drinks until he couldn't stand up. Sometimes he took me to parties with the Spanish gypsies. They cooked *paella* and played guitars and sang and danced flamenco until the sun came up. When he played with the Africans he stayed out late too and would come home with a plate of food and the most fabulous stories, sometimes a bracelet or a pair of handmade earrings or a wood carving of a fertility god that fit in the palm of my hand. But he didn't play with any of them for the money. He finally told me he had been receiving checks from his mother each month for his rent. He was just glad to be included and happy to play. When I went with him to parties, the women mostly ignored me but the men made plenty of conversation. He knew nationalists from Algeria, Cambodia, Vietnam, Morocco, Tunisia, Martinique, Guadeloupe, and Haiti.

"Have you heard anything about Olu-Christophe?" I asked.

"Not a word. I think for sure they sent him back. I know

he's a survivor, I just hope he's lucky. We've been through a lot together. He's the closest I have to a family. He's my brother and I miss him." Ving looked like a brave soldier surveying a great loss on the battlefield, like a boy trying not to cry.

"I miss him too," I said putting my arms around his neck.

Ving stepped away, and into character as my manager and dresser. He checked the clock on the wall then looked at me, admiring the costume he'd created for my Paris debut. "It's time."

Music drifted above the smoke and laughter and loud talk in the tiny bar. A dozen tables were heavy with elbows, strong cigarettes, and booze. Three women with long shiny hair leaned against the bar in sequined lowcut blouses and leather miniskirts, fishnet stockings and stiletto heels. They lit their cigarettes in unison. Watching, waiting. Their eyes searching the haze for customers. I stepped into the smoky blue light aimed at the tiny stage and stood in front of a huge old-fashioned microphone in the borrowed tight-fitting purple satin dress. My short, natural hair was hidden under a straight black wig with bangs. The fragrant white flower tucked behind my left ear. Red-painted lips, gold dust at the corners of my eyes, pearls of sweat on the tip of my nose. I hoped the makeup hid my fear. My legs atop the silver high heels suddenly felt weak, but then I took a deep breath and closed my eyes. I was back in Georgia in a small roadside juke joint. I opened my mouth again, and Billie Holiday came out. Testifying. "I'm a Fool to Want You." Confessing. "The End of a Love Affair." Declaring. "You Don't Know What Love Is." I cradled the microphone as

close as a kiss. The French called it playback. Lips in syn-
chronicity. A dozen tables watched the transformation. That
night I was Billie Holiday with every haunting look, roll of her
hip, tap of her foot, and lemon-scented fingers slicing the smoky
blue air. I was crying when the music stopped. The audience
was wild with appreciation, clapping, whistling, and cheering.
I closed my eyes and clicked my heels together, part of me wishing I was home.

"You were amazing." Ving met me at the edge of the stage
with a bouquet of yellow tulips and a kiss. "Why you crying,
baby?"

"I'm tired. Being in Paris is not how I thought it would be."
He held me and whispered that everything would be all right.

After my set I sat at the bar with the shiny girls and listened
to Ving play a mellow jazz set with a small group of musicians.
The buzz of the bar started up again.

Truth is, I was ready to go home, defeated that night. Two
days later Ving saved me by sending me to the south of France.
He had arranged for me to stay in a cottage on an estate being
looked after by artist friends of his.

"Maybe you'll get to meet Jimmy. Tell him I said hello."

There were train strikes all over the country and no one was
sure when the trains would be running again, so we went to an
agency that paired drivers and riders for a fee. It was an inexpensive way to travel, since the driver and I only had to split the
cost of gas and oil. I was paired with an amiable young Frenchman who sang along with the French pop tunes on the radio all
the way to Nice. I think he was taking speed because we
stopped only a couple of times for gas and toilet breaks.

I could say that my next few months in the south of France were paradise, like walking across the tops of tall, lush-leafed trees. I could say that I had tea on the terrace of Baldwin's old stone farmhouse at the bamboo-shaded welcome table, but those would be pretty lies. After spending eleven hours in a small car, traveling through the night, I was met in the town square in Vence by Ving's friend Prosper, the caretaker of the large estate in the hills above the town, and his boyfriend, Yanni. They were both artists, collaborators really. They worked on large abstract paintings in a converted barn. Prosper painted colorful landscapes for three hours in the morning, and Yanni worked on portraits of mythical animals for three hours in the afternoon. To make money they designed ceramic tiles with Matisse-style motifs and sold them in shops in the old part of the town. The main house on the estate was a sixteenth-century two-story gray stone building next to a silver-leafed olive grove. Yanni disappeared inside the stone house, and I followed Prosper, carrying my two bags down a rocky path on the far side of the olive grove. Prosper pointed to a shuttered wooden structure that he said housed a library and an art collection. I soon found myself alone in a small, bare one-room cottage overlooking a deep vine-choked gorge with a river gurgling deep inside of it. The cottage faced gray hills, beyond which was the village of St. Paul de Vence, where, Prosper told me, James Baldwin lived. I was happy for a while.

I would not have been lying naked on a sofa in an almost empty apartment in the chemin du Casse Pieds if I had not been hungry and the artist were not paying me so well. It was winter in the south of France.

"Here in Vence," the artist kept repeating, "the light is perfect."

I didn't know how he could see anything clearly, after drinking two beers at breakfast, a bottle of Burgundy at lunch, and even as I stood naked at the window in the glare of the noonday sun, he sipped from a huge snifter of cognac, wetting the corners of his wild moustache.

It was cold at night. The oil fuel tanks to heat my cottage were expensive. I reasoned that only if I ate salads all week could I afford to be warm. It was one or the other, food or heat. As I lay on the scroll arm of the backless sofa, its faded rose silk was sweet against my skin. The bare, dusty apartment was dim and cool behind me. The square below was empty. I didn't want to think about the dark stains under my elbow or the darker thoughts in the cesspool behind the artist's bloodshot gray eyes.

Jake was a big man with a head of thick white hair, grizzled like an old sea walrus and unsteady from all the alcohol he had consumed since sunrise. Earlier we had eaten on the town square under the plane trees with four Japanese artists just come from the Matisse Chapel and a Danish couple on an art-buying trip for a chain of international business hotels. The Japanese were excited by their visit and described it to us as if they had climbed a great mountain, and like Moses, seen a marvelous vision.

Jake had taken me to the chapel on the day I'd arrived at his table on the square looking for work as an artist's model. In

1941 Henri Matisse had moved to Vence to escape Allied bombing on the coast. He became ill and was nursed back to health by Dominican Sisters. As a gift of thanks he built and decorated for them the Chapelle du Rosaire, known locally as the Matisse Chapel. The white-tiled walls of the small chapel were embellished with simple black line drawings of the Stations of the Cross on which the sun filtered through enormous stained-glass windows, casting pools of yellow, blue, and green light. Matisse worked on the chapel well into his eighties, sometimes from his sickbed. I felt a holy presence as we walked around the room. In the silence I heard voices clear as church bells. *Take from me, the voices seemed to say, Take from me.* And as if I were watching a movie in fast forward, in the quiet beauty of the chapel I saw my life begin to take shape. I took out a piece of paper and scribbled every word I remembered and drew lines and dashes in places to show me the way there again. *A story is like a map.*

Jake also took me that day to a tenth-century cathedral in the old part of Vence. Inside the tiny chapel there was a Chagall mosaic, and Roman tombstones embedded in the walls. When Jake touched my arm to lead me around I felt a chill run down my spine. It felt like a warning, but I brushed it aside.

Jake was a successful artist. His work was sold in galleries in New York, New Mexico, San Francisco, and Los Angeles, owned by museums, art collectors, and dealers who visited his studio from around the world. He owned one of the old cream-colored villas on the square, where he lived and kept his studio and a small sculpture garden among the lemon trees.

"I must thank Monsieur Prosper. You will do fine." On that

first day I was shy, but he was patient. He asked me to stand at the window and look down on the square. I could hear the opening and closing of the camera shutter as I slowly wrapped around my head the large woven black-and-white tasseled scarf like the ones Arab men wear in the Middle East. My back to him, I lifted my arms to tie the ends. *Change.* I turned toward him, crossing my arms across my bare chest. *Change.* I kneeled in the dust and let my hands rest in my lap. *Change.*

Jake promised to introduce me to his friend Jimmy, a black American writer.

"Do you know his work? He's a nice guy. If I were to make a statue of Jimmy I'd cast it in gold."

He acted as if James Baldwin was his best friend. The hope of meeting my literary godfather was partial payment for lying naked on the rose silk couch stained with other women while Jake made poor excuses to touch me with the hand he used as a napkin at lunch. Jake was bad news. I knew this when he asked me casually if I was interested in doing an erotic art film for extra money. He called them erotic but they were nasty any way you looked at them. I watched five minutes of one of his friend's films before walking out of the dark room with the sound of their taunting laughter at my back. Erotic to him meant women humiliated, submissive, spread open for his pleasure. He knew I needed money, but I was not as desperate as that.

He took pictures of the sisters who worked as cashiers in the supermarket. They looked angelic in his photographs, like lovers lying in each other's arms. Their life-sized black-and-white photographs hung for all the world to see in his living room over his purple velvet sofa.

I wondered what my mother would think of her little girl if she saw me stretched out naked, mauled by the eyes of a drunken hairy beast. I wondered if she would have understood why I wanted to meet Baldwin so badly. Nothing had prepared me for that moment in that dusty room with cobwebs lacing the corners. At first I wondered if I would have to do battle with him and run naked down the marble staircase and into the square below filled with plane trees, old pensioners, and tourists sipping beer through straws. Jake was old and drunk and his hands shook so badly I was sure all of the images in the camera would be ruined. He had promised to give me one.

"You have to make sacrifices to be an artist," Indego had said the last time I saw him.

I will keep one of the blurry photographs to remind me of my sacrifice. Though my flesh will remember and though my flesh will fade away, my mind will remember.

We were Jake's girls. The Russian housekeeper with a mouthful of gold teeth, the teenaged sisters who worked as checkout girls, the middle-aged fishwife missing three fingers, and the pretty transsexual girl with whisper-thin eyebrows and huge breasts who worked in one of the bars on the square. Jake posed us like figures from his favorite paintings. One day I was the sleeping gypsy cradling a mandolin next to a stuffed lion in a moody blue Rousseau. The Moor in a Rousseau dream playing the flute while monkeys swung in the trees, lions prowled the woods, and the fleshy fishwife lounged naked on the sofa in a jungle. One day he paid a little boy to paint my naked body with blue and white polka dots like a Seurat. When he wanted to pose me like Greek statues headless, armless, my body mutilated, I became alarmed.

One morning at breakfast over a pitcher of beer and a plate of thick sausages and bread, a girl who looked as if she was in her late teens appeared at the table under the plane trees. She was Jake's daughter by his second wife. I could see the contempt she felt for her father. She tolerated him, and he treated her like one of his models.

She looked at me, surprised. "You're American. Are you one of Jake's girls?" Her father raised his glass of beer and interrupted her curiosity with a toast.

"To artists everywhere and their muses." He pushed himself away from the table and said he was going to take a piss.

"I'm a writer."

"So what are you doing hanging out with the old man?"

"I'm a poor writer, and your father pays models well."

"How long have you known Jake?"

"I've been modeling for him for a couple of weeks. He said he would introduce me to James Baldwin."

"Introduce yourself. Go over the hill to St. Paul de Vence. Ask anyone where Monsieur Baldwin lives. My father is a very manipulative man. Don't trust him. You're young and pretty, he'll take the advantage if you let him."

Jake's daughter had come for money, and when he stumbled back to the table she stayed just as long as it took for Jake to withdraw several large bills from his wallet and hand them over. She took the money and shoved it in the pocket of her blue jeans. When she pulled away from the curb the tires of her Jeep made a loud screeching noise.

Not long after that another visitor arrived to sit at our table. Jake bought a bottle of German beer for Jimmy's friend, an effeminate young man who carried himself with the grace of a ballerina. He wore a pale yellow scarf around his long scarred neck. He stayed only a few minutes and took only a few sips from the bottle of beer. Jimmy's friend said that Jimmy was not well, that he was not in St. Paul De Vence just over the hills from where we were sitting under the plane trees, but that he was in Paris working on an upcoming theater production of *The Amen Corner.* For a moment I panicked.

"Are you sure?" I asked.

The young man laughed and took another sip of beer.

"Positive, honey. He's gone," Jimmy's friend said. When he left, Jake and I were joined by some of Jake's regular drinking buddies—two well-dressed silver-haired Englishmen wearing blue blazers and colorful ascots knotted neatly around their wrinkled necks. I didn't model for Jake that afternoon. I slipped away unnoticed and walked back up the hill to my little cottage and sat down at my desk. I had come all this way to meet James Baldwin, hoping to learn from him some kind of secret about love and life and writing. I picked up the gold pen Dr. Bernard had given me, and between my tears words began to bloom on the page, one after the other. Words crowded each other, trying to lead me out of despair. I was exuberant. The maps I'd made were guides to my interior. I remembered all the places I'd been, all the things I'd seen, and I caught them in my imagination. Jimmy was with me and Langston too. I wrote to understand where I had been, where I was going, to make sense of the world that had led me to the small room on the edge of the abyss.

That night the mistral began. A strong, cold, dry wind that sounded as if the world were being blown away. Whistling as loud as a train traveling full speed. My fingers scratched out page after page. The terror was gone. I wrote down the things I was most afraid of: the maps of desire. Ving. The taste of need. Lucienne.

Prosper and Yanni came to check on me, but I sent them away. I wrote through the next few weeks, living on bread, cheese, black coffee, cigarettes, and wine, as the strong wind threatened to blow the house apart. I paced the floor, then wrote down a word: I washed the dishes as I looked out at the mountains in the distance, an image appeared and became a paragraph; as I lay half asleep in the candlelit room, a dream became a chapter that made all the other pages that came before it make sense.

One night I fell asleep facedown on the dozens of pages I'd written. In my dream someone was building a house underwater. I awoke to the sound of hammering. Someone was beating on the door. When I opened it Ving was standing there, as handsome as his music. I clung to him, kissing his face and neck.

Truly beloved.

This was not a dream. I had discovered something that no one could take away from me. I had found a path on my interior map and learned to follow it. There was power in the pen, I knew this for certain. I didn't need Jimmy to tell me that.

It was there all the time, just waiting for me.

witness

A BLACK GIRL IN PARIS was standing in the place where they stood.

On my last day in Paris I was a witness. I saw him from across the street on the boulevard St-Germain. His hair was short and graying, his skin ashen, large soulful eyes red and watery. He looked frail and weak. Aided by a young man in a suit, he walked unsteadily to the curb. The young man stood with his arm out, hailing a taxi in the light rain. My legs wouldn't move, my mouth wouldn't open. He looked up and noticed me across the street, standing in the middle of the sidewalk staring at him. Baldwin raised his hand and waved in my direction as if he had read my mind. Do you think I can do it too? Then he nodded and I thought I saw his lips moving over the words.

Yes, soul sister, you can do anything.

The light changed and I crossed the street to approach him. When I got near he took my hand and pressed it between his. His eyes wandered over my face and then to my hands. He kissed me on each cheek. Just then a taxi pulled up and his young friend helped him into it. As the taxi sped away I felt a hand on my shoulder. A white-aproned waiter stood beside me.

"The American, he is your friend?"

I nodded yes in a daze. "He left this." The waiter handed me a map of London and rushed back inside the restaurant. When I opened the map I realized that what I held in my hand was a treasure. Words were scrawled across the lines of the map like directions. They were so small and wild I could barely make them out, but it was as if he was speaking to me.

> *One word at a time*
> *story by story*
> *mile by mile*
> *let the sound of the voices carry you the distance*
> *welcome*

I went inside the cafe, sat down at his table, and smoked my last cigarette.

acknowledgments

Thanks, praises, and blessings to

the people

Aunt Lillian, Laura Pirott, Daniel A. Jones, Isabelle Bagshaw, Soul Sisters Salon: Pat Powell, Becky Johnson, Kate Rushin, and Carleasa Coates; Aunt Bobbye, Veronique Vaquette, Julie Siegel, Pearl Cleage, Debra Ginsberg, Rosemarie Robotham, Marje Salvodon, Wendy Belkin, Linda Bryant, Sharon Bridgforth, Kelle Ruden, Nina Shope, Paule Marshall, Robert Movradinov, Valarie Henry, Debra Brooks, Heidi Iratçabal, Billie Allen, Valerie Maynard, Ange Guillot, Kate Davenport, Laurence Perez, Anne Moutot, Ted Joans, Anasuya, Jason Weiss, Cathy McKinley, Nestor Pirott, Dorothea Smartt, Eve Humphreys, Nancy Buell, Alane Freund, Venus Irving Prescott, Veronica Chambers, Tina McElroy Ansa; the students who trusted me; librarians and postal workers everywhere; Sandra Dijkstra and her remarkable staff; Julie Grau, Hanya Yanagihara, and all the people at Riverhead who made this book possible; and especially Langston, Jimmy, Billie, and Josephine.

the places

The city of Paris, the town of Vence, The Karolyi Foundation, Charis Books & More, Saratoga Springs Public Library, the Writers Room and Yaddo and the people there, who make the house a home.

the things

that kept me going . . .

A room of my own, sweet potato pies, XXX, the magic angel pig, belly laughs, Aretha's fried catfish at Youngblood's restaurant in Atlanta, tickets to a WNBA game to see the NY Liberty win at home, XXX, the original ticket to Paris, bouquets of freesia, the grant from the American Aid Society of France, and basil, public libraries, cooking new recipes, independent bookstores, coffee, the phone calls to check on me, tea, magnolia blossoms, the Staten Island Ferry, love letters, XXX, lemon tarts, e-mail, checks in the mail, mile-high wigs, and five golden rings.

about the author

Georgia-born writer Shay Youngblood is the author of the novel *Soul Kiss* and a collection of short fiction, *The Big Mama Stories*. Her plays, *Amazing Grace, Shakin' the Mess Outta Misery,* and *Talking Bones* (Dramatic Publishing Company), have been widely produced. Her other plays include *Black Power Barbie* and *Communism Killed My Dog*. An Edward Albee honoree, and the recipient of numerous grants and awards, including a Pushcart Prize for fiction, a Lorraine Hansberry Playwriting Award, several NAACP Theater Awards, and an Astraea Writers' Award for fiction, Ms. Youngblood graduated from Clark-Atlanta University and received her MFA in Creative Writing from Brown University. She has worked as a Peace Corps volunteer in the eastern Caribbean, as an au pair, artist's model, and poet's helper in Paris, and as a creative writing instructor in a Rhode Island women's prison. She is a member of the Writers' Guild of America and the Dramatists' and Authors' Guild. She lives in New York City.